For Rob,

Seeing Red

Good luck with your writing! Enjoy,
Heidi

Heidi Brod

authorHOUSE®

AuthorHouse™
1663 Liberty Drive
Bloomington, IN 47403
www.authorhouse.com
Phone: 1 (800) 839-8640

© *2017 Heidi Brod. All rights reserved.*

No part of this book may be reproduced, stored in a retrieval system, or transmitted by any means without the written permission of the author.

Published by AuthorHouse   9/01/2017

ISBN: 978-1-5246-9175-2 (sc)
ISBN: 978-1-5246-9176-9 (hc)
ISBN: 978-1-5246-9174-5 (e)

Library of Congress Control Number: 2017907538

Print information available on the last page.

Any people depicted in stock imagery provided by Thinkstock are models, and such images are being used for illustrative purposes only. Certain stock imagery © Thinkstock.

This book is printed on acid-free paper.

Because of the dynamic nature of the Internet, any web addresses or links contained in this book may have changed since publication and may no longer be valid. The views expressed in this work are solely those of the author and do not necessarily reflect the views of the publisher, and the publisher hereby disclaims any responsibility for them.

Prologue

"Seraphina." The sound of my name, spoken as a dark whisper exploding in the night, terrifies me. With each new step, I regret my decision to walk home alone.

His voice sends a chill that buries itself deep in my bones. My breathing is ragged. My heart is pounding. Again he whispers my name; the weight of it hangs heavy in the cold night air.

I hear the echo of his footsteps first. A streetlight flickers like a firefly, distracting me, losing precious seconds I don't have to waste.

He is getting closer.

Snow and ice cover the ground near Harvard Square.

At first, the pain comes in quick cuts, like a movie, fast and hard. The force of the blows. The ache in my ribs. Eyes blurry.

The world tinted red.

Black shoes. Watery blue eyes.

Violence is hell, sharp like a razor blade. I am no longer connected. I'm energy and light, free from the pain coursing through my body. It recedes into a jigsaw puzzle of noises and fragmented images, now stored in the hard drive of my memory.

My body absorbs each blow.

"It's too late to be out in the dark alone. What a mess you are. What a mess you will be," he says, his breath stale and laced with alcohol.

I taste blood in my mouth. I'm paralyzed. All I can do is wait for it to end.

His hands are around my neck. I'm suffocating in the darkness.

"Please don't kill me."

"Be quiet."

My eyes closed.

"Will I?"

"Die today."

He shows no sign of mercy. Am I dreaming?

This moment, my misfortune is the axis my life turns on.

I'm screaming but without sound. His body is crushing me. *Please help me.*

Heavy breathing.

"Hickory dickory dock, the mouse ran up the clock," he chants.

Something wooden, heavy as a baseball bat, cracks my skull. There's no more pain. I'm numb.

The ground rises up, and my head hits the pavement. I lose consciousness.

One

SERAPHINA SWIFT

NOW

Iron is the traditional gift for six years of marriage. It is strong and resistant to fracturing. It is malleable yet durable, and it is indestructible.

None of these are words I would use to describe the current state of my marriage.

The nightmares started up again with the birth of my daughter, Sky. The intensity leaves me trembling and fragile, transporting me back to a blood-soaked alley in the dark recesses of my memory. Now I am feeling vulnerable, and vulnerable just isn't comfortable. My imagination is my cage.

Someone is stalking me. The truth gnaws at me like a nail buried deep in my bones.

Safe is an unattainable state. I'm sure other people don't feel this way. They are normal. I have accepted that I will never be a normal girl. I will always be haunted by the broken memory of trauma. I feel as if I've walked straight through hell and come out the other side into the blinding light of day.

I feel the weight of the gun in my hand.

"That's the Glock 42. It's a little big for you. You're tiny," he says, bringing me out of my daydream.

The guy behind the counter at the gun shop smiles as if I should be flattered. He could have used any other word—*thin, slender, petite*—anything other than *tiny*, which makes me more venomous. Those other words would have taken the edge off; instead he pours gas on an open flame.

"Try this gun instead. Ladies use it more as a summer carry. You can throw on a T-shirt and shorts and just run to the store. You're a virgin, right?"

I'm feeling on edge and jittery. My heart is pounding, and I'm having trouble breathing. It hurts to have a pulse. I want to die. I'm having another panic attack. I look away. I feel his eyes on me, and I see his mouth curl into a wicked smile.

His eyes wash over my body. I don't like the way this is going. Lately, I think I'm going insane; maybe Harper is right that I need to talk to someone.

"What?" I ask, letting myself be distracted by the coldness of the metal of the gun in my hand.

"Is this your first time in a gun shop?" he says.

I stare at the gun in my hand and realize I have forgotten to put on my wedding ring this morning. With so much on my mind, I rushed out of the house without it.

"No. It's not my first time. It's been over a month since you processed my permit application. I was in last week and this marks the end of my waiting period. I just need the gun and I'll go. Zack knows me. Is he here?"

"No. He's not here. I'm Jacob. I'm just filling in for him today. You really should try before you buy. We've got a range out back. Let me show you a few other options. What did you say your name is?"

"I didn't. It's Seraphina Swift."

I've been up all night with the baby, which makes it harder to focus on anything. I was alone again. Another night with a bottle of rosé in the backyard, just staring up at the stars, a blanket of darkness surrounding me.

"Hold on, let me check the back. He probably left it for you," Jacob says, taking out a black velvet tray with more guns and running his fingers over the chamber. I pick up a combat shotgun. It's larger and heavier. I'm in awe of its weight and power.

I'm not the girl I used to be, but at least now I know I'm still desirable. All of my damage is hidden from the world. The marks made by Harper are invisible. They have cut me a million different ways.

Jacob returns with my gun. "Sorry about that. Is this it?"

"That's the one." I say, as the world starts to move faster, grinding to pieces and spinning like a wheel.

"I don't think you're ready for this one, love. Not a lot in inches, but it's got a lot of power behind it, if you know what I mean." He winks and moves in closer, leaning over the glass counter, his eyes softening.

I can feel the color rise into my cheeks. I didn't come here looking for this kind of heat. I came here to buy a gun—one that I can use for protection.

A gift that's priceless, pure gold; one that I will wear on my body as if it is a necklace made of diamonds and pearls.

"Try this one. It's a Smith and Wesson. Just like Eleanor Roosevelt carried. She carried a .22-caliber gun."

My body is trembling. The adrenaline kicks in, coursing through my veins. The flashbacks always make me lose control.

It's as if my whole life is put on pause. Lately, it keeps happening, over and over. Every muscle is on high alert, seized, and on autopilot.

I can see his lips move, but I can't hear any sound. The silence stretches out in the space between us, as I lift the gun and aim it between Jacob's watery brown eyes.

And then I pull the trigger.

I hear the bullet explode from its chamber. *Bang!* Splatter. Scatter. The blood is everywhere.

I picture myself tearfully recalling the events for a news crew later. Just like the drama that played out on TV that frigid morning in Boston the night I was raped. I cannot break free from the night terrors or the jagged memories that shatter my sanity. I can't remember anything from that night. Now I have a bad habit of daydreaming in public, often mid-conversation. I indulge my daydreams. I get lost in them. Soon, I realize there is no blood or bullet, just a very pissed-off Jacob, waving his hands to get my attention.

"Whoa, you always do a safety check, make sure there is no mag, no bullets. You can't just pick up a gun, point, and shoot. Are you crazy?"

"Sorry. Almost an accidental discharge. But I'm guessing you know how that is, right, Jacob?" I say through gritted teeth.

I'm still wrapped up in the powerful sensation of finally pulling the trigger. I am used to handling men with big egos, like Jacob, but never with a gun, much less one that may have been fully loaded.

I know Harper will be the first to agree that his wife has gone crazy—and not just a little crazy. I have gone full-blown, bat-shit crazy. The darkness of my past has finally pulled me under, and I've given in to the pressure of it. The violent memories are taking me further away from everyone and everything I love most.

SEEING RED

Now, with a gun in my hand, I feel peace. I want revenge. I have found my safe place in the world. I have the strength I will need to fight back. I put the gun down. It feels heavy, even without the ammunition.

After all, Jacob is right: I am a virgin now, but not for much longer.

Jacob isn't going to stand in my way. He is a fool to think he has a chance with me anyway.

He reacts to my words as if they are made of steel, ripping at his flesh and exposing a bloody, open wound. I am angry in an obvious way. I gave up caring about what others might think a long time ago. The old Seraphina would run or shut down. The new Seraphina came to win. I focus only on the endgame. No distractions. This time, I make it clear with words that I don't need or want anything other than for Jacob to complete the transaction so I can be on my way.

"I'll pay for that in cash. I really need to go."

"Are you sure you're all right? Let me try to reach Zack," Jacob says, narrowing his eyes.

The fan hums from up above and the air around me is cool. All I can feel is heat, baking into my bones. Jacob is about to ruin my plans.

Tomorrow morning, I will disappear without a trace.

In the years since we married, Harper has become a prominent investigator with the district attorney's office. With so many high-profile cases, he made it easy for me to specify in detail the urgent need for self-protection.

Jacob's words cut through the heat of my emotions. "We have a range out back. You can practice. You need speed. You need accuracy. You need to know how to manipulate. Something tells me that you're a natural at manipulating."

Now his eyes are cold, dismissive. Jacob leans forward, and his soft smile fades into a sneer.

"Say I'm going to attack you, Seraphina."

I try to swallow the memories. I bite down on my tongue and taste the metal of my own blood. I fight to stay focused and present.

"You need to have your wits about you. You can't be lost in some daydream. And that thing in your hand, little girl, it may as well be a hammer and a bucket of nails. Chances are you put a nail through your hand before you figure out how to build a house all by yourself."

I pause for a second as the anger takes over. I am feeling unsteady. I can tell he is trying to reach me, to press my buttons with his misogynistic tone and attitude.

"It's not every day I get a celebrity in here, you know."

"What, I'm not …"

"I remember you. Zack told me all about you. You're that girl, right. The one from Harvard. Didn't you make national news when you killed him. It was self-defense, right? Can I ask you something?"

"Sure."

"If you killed him, why didn't you ever tell your side of the story? It's been years."

"I wanted to get on with my life," I say.

"Yeah, how's that going for you?" he asks, counting the cash.

"I'm fine."

"That's a lie. You're standing in a gun shop, having a panic attack."

I look outside. The heavy cumulus clouds tower in the sky, threatening to obscure the sun.

"I guess I'm not sure how my story ends, you know, who the bullet is actually for," I say with a bitter laugh.

"We don't sell pity here."

Thunder and lightning, the sounds of a heart breaking.

Jacob hands me a bag with the gun and ammunition.

I close the door on the gun shop. I will leave in the morning. I can imagine leaving all of this behind. Just me and Sky, starting over again, somewhere far away from Harper and his violence.

My mind is restless as I walk across the parking lot. I reach for the car keys in my pocket, but I'm distracted by a strange display of debris on the pavement, glass fragments everywhere, like tiny jewels.

As I move closer, I see a broken beer bottle next to the car door. I can feel a sharp pain above my eye, followed by a blinding headache.

My mind flashes back to that night in Boston. The shards of glass are sharp and jagged like a lethal weapon; the top glistens a deep sanguine color. I remember slashing at the air wildly. I remember trying to scream and fight for my life, but I couldn't make a sound.

I kick the bottle away and massage my temples from the dull pain. I slump against the car door, exhausted.

I open my purse and take out a pill. I swallow the Benzo dry and get in the car, resting my forehead against the coolness of the steering wheel.

I am haunted by the flashbacks. I struggle to connect the faint sounds, feelings, and memories to picture, like an inverted silent movie. I jump from a knock on the glass of the car window.

"Hey, you okay?"

"Fuck, Jacob. You scared the shit out of me," I say, my hand flying to my chest. I can feel my heart pounding.

"Sorry. You left your hat, and it's freezing out here. Listen, I'm sorry about what I said back there. It's your story, and it's none of my business, but I can tell you're in trouble. I think maybe I can help you."

"You asked me why I don't tell my story. I can't remember anything. I blacked out. I woke up in a hospital the next morning. Whoever committed murder is still out there. They've come back for me. I'm having horrible nightmares and flashbacks. I'm really scared."

"Let me help you. Let's talk about it. I'll get you a cup of coffee before you head back home?" he says, pointing to the All-American Diner across the street.

"I don't drink coffee."

"Tea?"

"Nope."

"Tequila?"

I consider his request. Finally, I put the key in the ignition. "Tempting, but no. I have to get home."

"Are you always like this? So distracted and intense?"

I nod.

"Listen, take my phone number. Sometimes things aren't as bad as you think they are."

I hate that as much as I hate it when someone says, "Smile."

"And sometimes they're worse," I say and give him my best sympathetic smile. I roll up the window. The car jolts onto the highway. I feel a tightening in my chest, like Jacob has taken all of the air with him. The sound of the tires on the road are like the beat of a drum. The rhythm does nothing to soothe my nerves.

My tank is empty; I need gas. I look around at the blank faces driving home, and I can't imagine anyone stopping to help me when my car runs out of fuel. All of these people are rushing home to something.

I feel so disconnected and off in my own world. The deep-red Japanese maple trees line the highway, and heavy gray storm clouds bloat up above as wisps of fog hang on the mist like smoke.

My eyes scan the cars around me. I notice someone has pulled out behind me, and they are weaving in and out to catch up. I switch lanes.

Someone is following me.

My pulse throbs in my veins. My muscles are tense and frozen in fear. I'm hyperventilating. Another panic attack. The broken bottle must have been a trigger.

With conscious effort, I calm my breathing.

Time ticks slowly. I put my foot on the gas. The stranger is still following me. I feel danger as the car moves closer, weaving in and out of traffic.

I turn on the radio, distracted and anxious to be going home to my sweet baby, Sky.

I don't see the light turn red. I slam on my brakes, but I am traveling too fast to stop.

My view is instantly consumed by the airbag. My eyes well up with tears. I don't expect the radio to keep playing, but it does, which makes the car crash feel more surreal.

"A Sky Full of Stars" by Coldplay is my soundtrack for destruction, mixed with a symphony of grinding metal and shattered glass.

I realize that somewhere in the dark places of my mind, I am still a freshman at Harvard, freezing, alone, and beaten in a dark alley.

I didn't fight back that day, and looking back now, I've been frozen and numb ever since.

After the crash, I can feel my body split into two people. The other Seraphina is some sort of an apparition perched on the trunk of the car, watching.

The hood is crushed like an accordion. Both of us are soon surrounded by an emergency crew.

I am locked in a heated stare with my dark shadow self; her smile starts to fade as she turns into a haze of fog and smoke.

I am either hallucinating or in the presence of an otherworldly evil, a harbinger of doom.

The stranger is gone. My eyes track the space around me. I remain frozen in pain and fear.

I have no words for what my life has become. Time feels heavily compressed and moving at the velocity of a falling body.

After the crash, there is the emergency crew and then the ambulance on the way to the hospital. Something about death—when you have cheated it as many times as I have, you start to make peace with the grayness of it.

I've already painted the picture in my mind of how it will look. I want my ashes blasted to the edge of space, so my soul is free to travel, soaring above wildflowers, mountaintops, and violet-tinted sunsets. I'm finally safe and awash in color and light.

This life has hurt me more than death ever could.

A call to Harper prompts his usual mix of concern and hostility. In all fairness, he has gotten the short end of the stick when signing up to be my emergency contact.

The attack has left me in a permanent state of emergency, often swinging between paranoia and fear. I can always imagine all of the things that can go wrong in the world, because in my world, just about everything has.

There is still a part of me that feels alive—the one that cheated death when it came to collect me, attempting to sever the last ties between body and soul.

I feel lost in the world. I can't find the part of me that stayed strong, the part that feels indestructible, even bulletproof; the part of me with the instinct to scream and fight back, to live and feel safe again.

I met Harper at Harvard. He was graduating at the top of his class. I had recovered as best I could from the attack, and all of the publicity surrounding the murder forced me to spend most of my time in the library.

I was hiding, still flailing and floundering in the chaos of recovery and self-doubt. I watched in awe while Harper soared, with no fear or limitation to what he could achieve. He drifted through life light as a feather, never burdened by the weight of things. When I was around him, something as easy as breathing became hard to do. Each time I saw him, he still took my breath away, crawling into that narrow space in my heart, cracking it wide open until he touched every part of me.

Harper's love, the pleasure and pain of it, felt like a reason to live.

Yes, this is what it was supposed to feel like, to know another's body, the way he knew mine.

Deep down, I wondered why he would pick a girl like me, with my damage on display. Something about me, dark hair and blue eyes, gave me an edge among all the Boston blondes.

I knew that night had changed me, and now all of my secrets had grown dark and rusted.

Maybe my darkness is what attracted Harper. The Boston bars were full of good girls named Laura, who had grown up inside white picket fences, feeling safe and protected. Those same girls were more than happy to roll over, open wide, and let him have his way.

Harper had never met anyone like me. I was touched by violence. It still flowed through me, threatening to crush the last bit of goodness in my soul, and something about that made our sex electric.

I was still disconnected and healing. My father always taught me to be strong and soldier on. I just put the memories in a little box, like a ticking time bomb waiting to explode. With Harper, I was free from the pain. I felt alive and completely in love, the kind of love that makes your knees shake. A love that is strong like metal, not weak like my flesh and bone.

We had our second date, already bloated on love and lust. Harper piloted a plane to Martha's Vineyard. The ride with him was always thrilling.

That day, he decided he would make me his match. We drank wine on the silk rug, listening to Louis Armstrong and Coltrane on vintage vinyl. I had never met anyone like Harper. He was alpha, razor smart, and thrill-seekingly insane.

With him, I feel naked. Everything is uncovered and exposed for him to see. I was able to move forward and forget the past. I was the funnier, more beautiful and lighter version of me. The one I was born to be. We sheltered ourselves from those around us who settled, the ones who couldn't wait to find their true soul mate. We built a wall around our love, brick by brick, until we had a fortress.

With Harper, I felt safe and protected for the first time. For him, I was the match that set fire to his all- star image, threatening to burn it all up.

Two

HARPER SWIFT

The approach of the ferry is made more evident by the chaos of the crew and the cutting of the engine.

Harper asks the bartender, "Do you have a light?"

"You can't smoke in here. Sorry."

"Okay. Can I still borrow the light?"

Yes, there is something wrong with me. I can't stand being with other people.

Harper's charcoal eyes dart back and forth. He clearly doesn't want another altercation with the steward.

He makes his way toward the deck, and he stops and lights a cigarette. He remembers he quit last month, or at least that's what he told her. He cups his hands around the cigarette and takes a deep drag, again and again, until he feels a warm sense of peace wash over him.

He lets the smoke swirl and fill up his lungs. He blows a cloud out into the open air, and webs of smoke spread out in a haze over the wooden planks.

Harper stares out at the trees, the bridge hidden from his view, the water a sapphire blanket that remains still.

With Seraphina, nothing is ever easy. Something about her radiates toxicity and unhappiness. She needs help but refuses to talk to anyone. She keeps fighting him. He worries about leaving her alone with Sky. She is just a baby. He will insist that she see a doctor and insist on a diagnosis and medication, or he will have to leave, for the sake of his child. Seraphina's night terrors are escalating, along with her delusions and paranoia.

His gaze drifts to the rippling water. He feels cold and detached.

He will choose happiness, even if it means moving on. Would she be waiting for him on the dock again tonight? He can see her clearly in his mind, that same floral dress and pallid glow, waiting to have the last word.

Lately, she defies him at every turn. More than anything, he loves his job and he is good at it. He believes in justice above all else.

Now, when he is finally at the apex of his career, it is just like Seraphina to threaten to send it all up in flames with her paranoia, anger, and irrational fears.

He runs his fingers through his shock of wavy black hair, the chiseled lines of his jaw adding a piercing intensity. Seraphina's unhappiness is a catalyst for him and an impetus for him to start over.

He stamps out his cigarette and brushes an ash from his starched blue collar. Harper catches a glimpse of himself in the window. He watches the water below swell and billow, mesmerized by its rhythms. Secretly, he doesn't care about her problems. He just wants to be free from her negativity.

His phone starts to ring in his back pocket. It's Seraphina. He lets it go straight to voicemail and then plays it back. He wants to avoid another confrontation.

SEEING RED

On the voicemail, she is babbling incoherently. "Harp, I'm not crazy, even if I'm slowly driving you crazy. I can prove that I'm in danger and that someone is stalking me and our family."

At first, Harper thinks it's another one of her games, her manipulations, and he will return home to find her sauced and passed out on the kitchen floor while Sky sleeps peacefully in her bedroom.

He is about to hang up when he hears Seraphina say, "I'm in the hospital, Harp. I need stitches. You have to come now. You have to listen to me. We're all in danger, real danger. Help me before it's too late."

He feels like this is just drama for the sake of drama. He has given Seraphina so many chances. He still loves her deeply, but something inside him is breaking. He has Sky to think of. He has been responsible for holding their family together this past year.

Yet something in her voice tonight gives him pause. He can hear the fear, and it's palpable. He wonders if someone is stalking his family. The mystery of Seraphina's attack in Boston still haunts her. It didn't seem possible that she could have committed murder, even if it was in self-defense. It doesn't add up. She remembers only fragments and pieces from that night. Harper will never forgive himself if someone is hunting Seraphina and his family is in danger. For the sake of Sky and his sanity, he needs to abort his decision to finally move forward with a divorce.

He is, once again, plunged into a deep depression, and feelings of being trapped in his marriage and the depths of Seraphina's insanity. He is stuck in a middle-aged state of stasis.

His thoughts drift back to that night in the city when their marriage was bright and shiny new.

He had just gotten a promotion, and they had moved into the loft in Tribeca. It was August, summer's end, and their bodies were knotted in the morning sun.

The jade-green light in her eyes ablaze, her beauty possessed a potent alchemy.

He can still feel her fingers down his back, setting fire to his skin. He had her every way imaginable, the stone rough, cutting through her skin. They both believed marriage meant forever. For Seraphina, forever wasn't enough. At least she had said so in her vows.

That night, she let him consume her—breasts, legs, hips, hands, and thighs, enveloped in their heat.

But when the summer ended, she started getting colder, retreating into the same dark places. All of her promises were forgotten. Harper wasn't someone who accepted loss. He had lost her a little at a time until she had come undone.

Like a flame, he watched the darkness at the center consume the brightest part of Seraphina.

Now, most nights, if he comes home at all, it is to Seraphina staring out the window at the deep-blue water, at the boats that rise and fall along the Navesink River. He realizes that to most people, they have the fairy tale.

He isn't sure what is happening inside Seraphina that is tearing it all apart.

The drizzle thickens to drops, and the sun is starting to fade by the time Harper arrives at the hospital. He walks down the corridor.

He doesn't bother stopping at reception, and the receptionist doesn't bother stopping him.

A doctor pulls open the door and stumbles over the words, "You can follow me. Your wife is going to be just fine."

Harper responds with a nod and a handshake. "Can you give us a minute alone?"

SEEING RED

Outside the hospital window, the sun is sinking behind the trees.

"Are you all right?" Harper asks as he closes the door.

"Someone was following me. I saw him. I was trying to get away. I didn't even see the light turn red."

"I spoke to the police and nobody was there. It's just your imagination, *again*. You need help."

"You still don't believe me. So what, are you saying I'm crazy?"

"What did you take, Seraphina?" he asks angrily.

"Isn't that how you like your women? Diagnosed and heavily medicated? It wasn't my fault."

"It never is. They found a gun in your glove compartment. Can you explain that to me?"

"What? I have a permit."

"That is not the point or the question, and you know it. Don't play games with me, Seraphina. I'm not in the mood. You are sick. You need help."

"I'm not crazy. Someone is stalking me. They are hunting our family. They are out there every night, watching and waiting. Why can't you believe me? You're constantly questioning my sanity instead of helping me. Our family is in danger."

"I'm working. How many fucking times do I have to tell you that before you believe me? You're paranoid. The night terrors are getting worse."

"Maybe you're making me crazy. Where the fuck are you every night? You're not at home. Maybe you're just done with me and ready for a new, hotter, younger model. I'm starting to think that maybe you're the one that wants me dead."

"You're acting crazy again," Harper says.

"Why won't you listen to me? I saw that boat again last night. It was less than five hundred yards away from our dock. I thought

I got a picture, but it's gone. Someone must have hacked into my e-mail account and wiped out everything on my phone. I saw someone watching me from the boat. I can feel his eyes on me at night."

"After how many drinks? I'm surprised you're not seeing unicorns. I'll hire more security for the house. I'll put in a better alarm system. Whatever you need to feel *safe*. You are a mother. Start acting like one."

"I'm not crazy."

He won't look at me.

"You are so anxious and manic. I have no idea what kind of pills you're taking or what you even do all day. You've stopped working. You're not healthy and you have to talk to someone."

"I'm a mother. I'm with our child every day. You may not take it seriously but I do. Someone is stalking our family, and all you can think of is how it affects you. You are so selfish. I can't believe I never noticed that before. Why don't you try coming home and acting like a husband and a father? Until then, the only person I need to talk to is the bartender at Murphy's."

"This isn't a joke," he says angrily, his veins bulging.

He hands me a card. It reads, Dr. Gordon Ellis, Psychoanalyst. "Either you make the appointment or I can't do this anymore." Harper says.

"Well, I can't do this either. I can't have this conversation again. Our family just isn't a priority anymore to you. Is it, Harper?"

"I'm sorry, but you keep fighting me. I'm not going to do this with you. Not today. Not here. A girl was murdered, a college freshman and she was somebody's daughter, like Sky. That's a real problem. I have people counting on me for answers."

His words are like the sharp end of a knife. They keep twisting.

"What about our family? Don't you think we're counting on you? You're home late every night, that is if you come home at all. We need you. I need you."

"That's not fair. I've given you everything. *Everything*, and you're still not happy. Most of the time, you're not even thinking clearly. Everything you're running from—it's all in your mind. Can't you see it's just your imagination? When are you going to realize that? I'll drop you at home, but I have to get back to work."

"Maybe if you're lucky, I'll just disappear and you can get on with your life as if we never happened."

He's horrible. I hated him for my own vulnerability. My words play back in my mind. I sound like an unlikable, spoiled child who is well on her way to becoming an unlovable adult.

A young emergency room doctor with a nervous bedside manner is waiting to examine me.

He tries to focus on the fresh wound but keeps getting distracted by my old scar. I surprised him with a car accident. The doctor is craning his neck, rubbernecking, so he has to acknowledge it.

"That's a pretty nasty scar. What happened?"

"It's nothing. An old wound," I say while staring intently at Harper.

"Are you all right, Mrs. Swift?"

"I don't think so. I want to talk to the police. I need to know who was in the car that was following me. Did they get the license plate? Are they going to investigate?"

"Mrs. Swift, you've just been in a car accident, and that is traumatic. We can give you something to relax."

"Someone followed me home. I'm sure of it. It's not all in my head. It can't be."

"You're going to need some stitches, but other than a few bumps and bruises, you're going to be just fine. You really are lucky."

Lucky isn't a word I would ever use to describe myself.

"I called my plastic surgeon. We'll wait. Thanks, Doc," Harper says.

"God forbid I fuck up a photo op, right, honey? You can sew me up. I don't feel like waiting."

The distance between Harper and me is expanding faster than the speed of light.

"Or maybe I'll just do it myself at home with a needle and thread."

It grows wider than the space between two galaxies. "Thanks, we'll wait for the plastic surgeon. Forgive my wife; she's not herself today."

"This *is* who I am now, Harper. And it's who we are together that's made me this way," I say with a bitterness that even shocks me.

I see the nurses passing and I feel confused. I can't clear my mind. Even the air is oppressive, and I'm feeling jaded and bitter. I'm twisting, lost in the darkness.

"Where were you last night, Harp? Or this morning when the nanny showed up late?"

"I slept in the guest house. You are keeping me up all night with your nightmares. It isn't good for the baby."

He is begging me. I can hear the sadness in his voice. He's holding back his crocodile tears. I'm tired of his manipulations and lies.

"I know you're having an affair," I say.

I close my eyes and the feeling of sadness takes over, it grows and spreads out around me like a shadow.

"That's just not true. Everything I do is for you and Sky."

For Harper, his narcissism and hubris often shelter him from seeing the painful truth. He can't imagine that my unhappiness has anything to do with the state of our marriage. It's true, our love is fading, but it is a love built on trust that once burned so brightly and so passionately, it could spark a flame. They say time is supposed to heal, but I can see his heart breaking from my pain.

Neither of us notices the surgeon arrive. He looks uncomfortable as he preps the Novocain.

"I don't need that," I say.

"That's silly. Why put up with pain if you don't have to?" the surgeon says, looking at Harper for guidance.

"I have an unusually high tolerance for pain," I say, glaring at Harper.

Harper just nods to the doctor.

The look in his eyes says it all: he knows his girl all too well.

I don't just tolerate the pain. My body craves it. It has become my addiction.

On the ceiling hangs a poster: ONE MUST UNLEARN THE CONSTELLATIONS TO FINALLY SEE THE STARS. I look out the window at the stars burning fearlessly, brilliant and beautiful.

Each stands alone, a burning light of eternal energy and fire.

As the doctor spreads out his sterile instruments, my mind scratches and claws at the details from my past that stalk me.

Harper holds my hand. I watch the thread as it goes into the needle. The needle pierces my skin.

Pain is like Novocain; it soothes my broken heart. The stitches go in, one by one.

It is inevitable: the hospital reminds me of the violence of the night I was attacked and the fate of my recovery.

I woke up at Mass General in a hospital room like this one, my head aching, heart palpitating, body wrecked from the trauma, bandaged and bruised.

In the darkness, time vanishes and hope disappears into the night. I don't have many reliable memories from that night, just a bunch of fragments, carefully woven into a distorted patchwork of images, thoughts, and disconnected feelings.

Luckily, the CT scan ruled out a brain hemorrhage. Someone had turned on the television; my crime scene played out on the local news.

As I watched the images flash across the screen, my eyes were drawn to the beautiful weeping willow above the decaying garbage. I can still smell it rotting. The yellow tape that marked the crime scene wrapped around the base of the tree, draped over the branches like lights on a Christmas tree.

They had found his body while taking out the trash. The body was slashed with a broken bottle, and the crime scene was a bloody mess.

The night started just like any other. It was Halloween, a moonless, pitch-black night. I was working late at Johnny's Bar, serving drinks, when the room started spinning like a top. I walked outside to get some air.

"Are you all right?" my manager, Mike, asked.

"I think I'm sick. I've gotta go," I said, the world starting to whip and whirl around me. My whole body was tired, as if I were sleepwalking through sand, detached.

"Hold on. We close in five. Hang out and I'll walk you."

"I'll be all right. It's not far. I think I would rather just go."

Sometimes the wrong choices bring us to the right places, but not this time. This one took me straight to hell.

The flood of the streetlight streaked like the tail of a comet. It lit up the world around me, as if setting it on fire. The costumes and faces seemed to melt together, like wax into a searing, demonic scream.

I thought my eyes must be playing tricks when the light around me started to bounce and float like a meteor shower. The sparks were rising up from the street, like a firestorm. That's when I realized I had been drugged.

I walked quicker now, too far to turn back.

I cut through Cambridge Square and took the short cut through a dark alley, off Quincy Street. That was when I heard his whisper, exploding in the night.

My heart beat fast, like the beating of a drum. My breath, shallow with fear, sent a cloud of steam into the night air.

Snow and ice covered the ground near Harvard Square.

I turned to see his mask, the black cloak and hood of his costume, the angel of death. Something wooden and heavy cracked my skull. I fell onto the concrete, and that was when I lost consciousness, as if I were frozen in my own body—a witness to my own destruction.

At that moment, I saw the broken bottle with the jagged edges. I grabbed it and started cutting, slashing wildly, and connecting. The anger flowed through me—and the will to live.

The police found his body behind a dumpster in the alley. He had been stabbed repeatedly with a broken bottle.

At first, I felt a deep sense of gratitude that the evil visited upon me that night, the soul that floated up from the depths of hell, had been brutally murdered and I was alive.

I can still see his eyes in my dreams, and they are cloudy and dark. His eyes haunt me.

I was never a sweet child, but now I had succumbed to something volatile and dangerous.

There was too much blood at the crime scene. Even though I was the victim, I was treated like a criminal.

I can't remember most of it, and I can't imagine I could be capable of murder. Was someone else there that night? Could it be the same person who is stalking me now?

Harper squeezes my hand harder. The memories layer one on top of the other. I had never been hurt like that before. A blow to the ribs. Something sharp, like broken glass, twisted, cut deeper.

I was suffocating, existing in that space between life and death.

A week later, the torso of Ashly Barthel washed up in a burlap sack on Deer Island, throat slashed with a similar pattern of cuts on the body as the ones made to the man who attacked me. The killer had used a knife and not a broken bottle. He removed the heart and sent it with a series of taunting letters to the press and investigators.

The killer included a detailed anatomy drawing in pen and ink on paper, depicting a woman in two superimposed positions with her arms and legs apart, inscribed in a circle and square, the image crudely resembles da Vinci's *Vitruvian Man*.

Each cut from the attack was intricately drawn and premeditated. He was an organized killer, and he was still out there. I couldn't get investigators to listen or reopen the case.

I was convinced I was just a pawn, the poor dog he used to throw off the scent, and somehow the murder of Ashly Barthel and the night I was attacked were connected. The media gave him the nickname "Renaissance Killer."

I know the truth of who committed murder that dark night I was attacked in the alley, a truth that is buried somewhere deep in my unconscious mind. It is a truth that leaks out in sounds and distorted images like brushstrokes on a canvas. I'm stalked by his watery blue eyes and haunted by the sound of his voice and the feeling that someone is always watching me.

I know he's still out there, waiting for me to step into the darkness alone again, so he can drag me under.

Another stitch. Blood-red anger flows through me onto Harper, threatening to drown us both. I can't run from it. I can't cut it off, like a limb. I carry it with me like a ticking bomb waiting to explode.

SEEING RED

The Christmas trees and decorations light up the night like a fairytale town. A flurry of snow has started and already dusts the ground in white satin.

Harper drives me back to the house in silence. The light from the pool house reflects on the river.

The koi pond is covered in a layer of ice and snow.

I watch Harper drive away; not even a car crash will keep him home for the night.

I blame him for leaving me alone, left running from the thoughts that rattle and shake me.

I try to remember our life before the suburbs; before the sleepless nights, the drinking, and the arguments. Now I'm feeling lost, alone, and giving up on a love that was once my addiction, his body as essential as the salt in my tears.

I enter the house quietly.

"Baby girl's asleep," says Birdie, our nanny, never looking up from her prayer book. "Now don't you go and wake her up again."

Tonight, Birdie looks old and frail. I watch her fingers scan the pages; her hair, thin and wispy as the night mist, is coiled high in a bun. Birdie was my shadow mother. She raised me, filling in the holes where a mother's love should be. Now she loves my daughter with the same grace and quiet strength of autumn rain.

I walk quietly into Sky's room. The lavender print of the wallpaper wraps me in warmth. The ceiling is hand-painted, a spring sky with clouds and butterflies in flight.

I peek into her crib, seeing tiny hands that tug at my heart and a shock of fire-red curls, her eyes wide open.

"I'm here, baby girl," I whisper.

Sky breaks into a toothless grin. There is nothing like this feeling, a love like oxygen. She is such a big miracle for such a small child. Sky won't take her eyes off me. It's as if she is afraid to look away.

Like she knows, in the blink of an eye, her mother may just disappear forever.

I take Sky in my loving arms and rock her gently back to sleep.

I start to sing softly: "Somewhere over the rainbow, way up high. And the dreams that you dreamed of, once in a lullaby."

Before long, she is fast asleep, and I put her down in her crib on the soft Chenille sheets. I catch my reflection in the mirror over the antique dresser. I run a finger over my jagged new scar. I lean in closer to the glass. No make-up; dark circles.

My face is cut into pieces, like a Picasso. Red slashes, distorted, disconnected; a river of blood flows through it.

I close my eyes and remind myself that I am a survivor, even if he is still out there, watching my every move. I will find out the truth, and I will survive for the sake of my child. I breathe deeply, in and out.

When I open my eyes, I am startled by Birdie standing behind me.

"Now I told you I've got her, but Ms. Sera, who's got you?" she says, looking at the fresh wound and the stitches.

"I'm okay. It's just a few stitches. I saw him today. He was driving, and he kept weaving in and out of the lanes. The police didn't catch him, but I'm sure of it. We're in danger, and Harper doesn't believe me. I'm not crazy. I'm not paranoid. You have to believe me. We have to protect Sky."

Birdie says, "All of your ghosts are in the past. Let them rest, Seraphina. Look at the dark circles under your eyes. You need rest. You can't live like this. You're going to get sick. It's time they stop haunting you." She takes me in her arms.

"You don't believe me either, do you, Birdie?"

"I'll be going to bed. I left dinner for you downstairs. You need to eat. You have to start taking better care of yourself, Ms. Sera," she says.

"Thank you, Birdie. Good night."

I make my way down the stairs to the wood paneled library. I open up a bottle of rosé, strikingly pale pink, like the blush of a newborn's cheek. The rush hits me all at once, savory and crisp.

It is the taste of my first summer in Montauk with Harper. The lull of the soft waves and the salty air as he slips his fingers underneath my bikini bottom and gently caresses me, until every inch of my flesh aches for him.

We dance on the dock under the crescent moon as it hangs over the harbor. White ships bob and glide on the water.

I pour myself another glass, this one more generous, half the bottle gone.

The snow has stopped, and it is a crisp, cloudless night. As I look out over the sweeping views of Seablades Estates, I turn the business card Harper has given me over and over in my mind.

That night, I dream of watery blue eyes in the shape of bullets, steel and sharp. I'm running through a labyrinth of hallways, lost and alone, feeling trapped.

I find a door and push my way out.

The sky is lit up, as if it is on fire. I look down, and my hands are covered in blood.

Three

BROOKE BECK

Wednesday night, 8:00 p.m. A small shrine of flowers sits on the steps of the brownstone where Brooke Beck had been raped and murdered. Harper knew it was going to be a bad one when he saw Detective Patrick Belle doubled over and holding his stomach, supporting his enormous frame on the hood of a patrol car. Belle is a towering, beefy man with a gentle manner and a Brooklyn accent, and a master of surveillance and studying human behavior. He has the steel-trap mind of a card counter. He was running the FBI's Behavioral Science Unit before Harper ruthlessly poached him.

Harper gets out of his SUV and walks past the police cars and the crime-scene-unit van.

"Why are you out here, Belle?" Harper says, sweeping behind him and up the stairs of the townhouse.

Belle shakes his head. "I needed air. The body is mutilated beyond recognition."

Harper ducks behind the black-and-yellow tape that says CRIME

SCENE DO NOT CROSS and steps into the brownstone, heading up to the third floor. He gags from the smell of the decaying body as he enters the apartment, sunlight pounding through the skylight. Harper takes a pair of latex gloves and puts them on. He can hear the sounds of the strobes and noises from the crime scene crew as they do their work.

"Has the medical examiner been here yet?"

"A long time ago. Where have you been?" Belle asks.

"At the hospital. Seraphina got into a car accident. She'll be fine. What happened here?"

"No sign of forced entry. She knew him and probably even let him in. No one heard any screaming. She must have been unconscious or drugged when they started cutting."

"Security?" Harper asks.

"Virtual. All cameras disabled. No tape."

Harper stops at the top of the stairs and is spellbound by a piece of South African art hanging on the wall. "What college student can afford to rent a townhouse in Harlem?"

The hallway walls are lined with African masks, and not the kind that look like you could pick them up in the airport gift shop.

The scene is raw and bloody, and the smell is hard to take. Fingerprint powder generously blankets the area.

Harper carefully avoids the section of the floor that is spattered with blood, as he moves in closer to examine the victim's remains. A framed picture on the wall shows Brooke Beck, early twenties, pale skin and beautiful.

The victim was raped and beaten. She is nude, lying on her back, with multiple stab wounds and her arms and legs apart. The blunt trauma rendered her head and face unrecognizable. She wears a gold chain with a cross on it, draped across her neck. The victim's heart has been removed.

Above her bed, Harper sees a drawing of the Vitruvian Man by Leonardo da Vinci in pen and ink. His mind goes back to the Boston murders, and he wonders if Brooke Beck's murder is somehow connected to the Renaissance Killer.

Belle takes a tub of Vicks VapoRub out of his pocket and puts a little under each nostril, an old cop trick that covers the stench of death. He enters the bedroom. A large flat-screen TV hangs on the wall. Harper notes the two antique mirrored side tables that are open and empty.

Other than an ornately carved mahogany bed with tall posts covered in white linen curtains for privacy, the place doesn't look lived in. Brooke Beck didn't have any of the usual family portraits or graduation pictures.

The word *slut* is written on the mirror in blood.

"She hosted a party here on Tuesday night. She was last seen by her friend Jessa Dante around midnight. When the apartment started to smell, the neighbor called the super, who notified the police; we entered through the ground terrace. He had to have a certain degree of skill to pull off incisions like that. None of the adjacent organs are damaged."

"Any family?" Harper asks.

"Estranged from the mother. Father was never in the picture. The neighbor says her boyfriend had a very possessive streak and that she was trying to break up with him," Belle says.

Belle takes out an evidence bag and hands it to Harper. It contains a dark-brown pod, about an inch long, rounded ends, rough but also shiny and polished on top, with a scar along the edges and a hole drilled in the center.

"Looks like some sort of spice," Harper says as he watches them place the remains of Brooke Burke into the plastic body bag.

"Someone really wants us to think this is a ritual killing. It almost feels staged."

Outside the brownstone, a crowd has formed, along with the television crew and a few locals posing for the cameras. Belle would deliver the usual vague information and half-truths for the obscene amount of coverage that Brooke Beck's case would get on the local news the next day, about a white girl brutally slain in Harlem the night before.

"Let's set up a candlelight vigil outside with surveillance and a press conference. ID everyone that comes through here, and offer a reward to anyone who can get us information on the boyfriend." Harper scans the gruesome scene and takes it all in. "Anything else I need to know?"

"Her Facebook page says she's bisexual. Sounds like Jessa Dante was her roommate and lover until a few months ago, when she moved out."

"Okay. You handle Jessa," Harper says.

They head out and back down the stairs.

"Sure. Say, you wanna grab some pizza real quick?" Belle says.

"What? Do I want to grab some pizza? Seriously, pizza? How the hell do you do that?"

"What? You prefer Chinese?"

"How can you even think about food at a time like this?"

"Well. You know that I can always think about food."

"Yeah, but that's disgusting. My stomach is churning right now."

"The answer is no, boss. That's all you have to say."

Harper holds back the laughter as they open the door to the brownstone, spilling onto a street full of eager eyes; dozens of journalists swarm them, every one looking for a headline.

"Was she raped?" a voice breaks through from the back of the crowd.

"Do you have an arrest?"

"We have no comment," Harper says as he moves confidently and gracefully through the crowd.

He slept at the office that night, woke up early, and went to the gym. He needed to run, burn off some of the toxic energy he'd been carrying around.

That and a shower would help to balance his mind's unrest.

Feeling better after a shower, he grabs his usual scrambled eggs and toast, while watching the local news.

A beautiful anchor with a sobering tone delivers the details of Brooke's murder.

Harper sees his face flash across the screen. His cell phone rings.

"Belle?"

"You're not going to like this."

"I'm listening," Harper says.

"The team tried to crack the encryption on the hard drive but triggered some sort of self-destruct mechanism."

"Did they get anything off it before it crashed?"

"In the last month, she's been active on Websleuths.com and Reddit and just about every other dedicated forum for Internet sleuths. Or 'bottom feeders,' as you always call them."

Harper hated amateur detectives. He figured they did more harm than good, poring over crime scenes and evidence. It was Facebook for the dead.

"Harp, you remember the Deer Island murders?"

"The Boston Harbor murders? That case has been cold for over five years."

"Cell phone records show Brooke contacted the Massachusetts State Police the day she was murdered and said she had found him, the

Renaissance Killer. Even had evidence to prove it. I went through all of the records from Boston."

"Did you find anything?"

"The last victim, Helena Achlys, cause of death was cardiac arrest. The toxicology report showed that she was poisoned by Ouabain."

"What is Ouabain?"

"It's a poison that is extracted from *Acokanthera* plants found in eastern Africa. The arrows are dipped into the concentrated liquid and used for hunting and warfare."

Belle pauses, his nerves raw.

"Harp, the body was found in the woods. She was shot with a crossbow, using the arrow poison. She was hunted, like something out of medieval times."

"Jesus," Harper says as he takes a deep breath in, haunted by the image of it.

"She had been given *Atropa* belladonna eye drops, an herb that is toxic and causes delirium and hallucinations. The name *Atropa* comes from *Atropos*, one of the three Fates in Greek mythology, meaning 'pretty woman' because the herb was used in eye drops to dilate the pupils of women's eyes to make them appear seductive. The Renaissance Killer took credit and sent photos from the night of the murder and a sketch of a crossbow, an old illustration by Leonardo da Vinci, to the media. Jessa Dante only wants to speak to you."

"Why?"

"She's scared."

"Fine. Text me the address. What else?"

"We spoke to Brooke's neighbor, Greg Callum. He said we should talk to her boyfriend. I can't find anyone who has laid eyes on this guy. Nothing on any of the tapes. It's like he's a ghost. The vigil is set for tonight."

Harper realizes they are dealing with a sophisticated killer, one who has established a complex system to destroy the evidence.

"So where do these dime-store Internet detectives come from? It's like a bad episode of *CSI*."

"Everywhere. They're just regular people off the street. Your trainer at the gym or the girl that cuts your hair."

"I guess. It's just pretty fucking creepy."

"One more thing, Harp."

"I'm listening."

"Well, you know the profile of these hobbyists, too much time on their hands. These web sleuths are obsessed with cases that suck up media attention. You know, like Caylee Anthony, JonBenét Ramsey, the big ones."

Harper nods. "Sure."

"A whole bunch of these people, including Brooke, are obsessed with you and Seraphina—well, your family, and the night she was attacked. And lately, there has been a lot of chatter online and in the crowdsourced forums."

"Really? The DIY detectives think they're on to something? Like what?" Harper says, feeling his defenses go up. He will always protect Seraphina. She has lived through a nightmare, and he won't allow anyone near her with intentions of having her relive the horror of the night she was attacked; not now, not ever.

"They have a witness. Someone who worked at the bar in Boston. They said they saw you leave the bar right after Seraphina on the night she was attacked," Belle says.

"So, what, they think I raped my wife?"

"No, Harp. They think you killed the man who did. They think by the time you caught up to Seraphina, the damage was done, and she couldn't have possibly inflicted that kind of damage on another man. She's not strong enough."

Harper laughs but then realizes Belle is serious.

"It wasn't me. I didn't follow her home. That's creepy. This is insane, Belle. Shut these people down, or I will. Get me everything from forensics as soon as it comes in. I'm on my way to see Jessa Dante."

Harper is furious. These days, anyone with a computer can consider themselves an amateur detective. He had checked out the chat rooms and all of the websites and considered them nothing more than ambulance-chasing ghouls.

Although many had the best intentions, most opened up a darker side—criminals who hid behind the safety of their own computer; predators, sex offenders, and serial killers. These websites are an incubator for evil, a scourge on society that should be undone.

The key-locked elevator at 59 Greene Street in SoHo opens up into a sprawling loft. The Corinthian cast-iron columns and wraparound ten-foot-high windows are breathtaking, but nothing compares to the beauty of Jessa Dante.

"Jessa?"

"Hi, Harper. Come on in."

She is stunning, radiant, with red hair and a tight, sculpted body. Her eyes blue and luminous.

"I'm Harper Swift. I'm sorry about Brooke."

"Thanks, and thanks for coming down here to see me." The travertine-tiled floors sparkle. The white lacquer walls pop with colorful, modern art.

In the corner are some storage boxes with books, waiting to be unpacked.

"Nice place. Have you lived here long?"

"A couple of months. Can I get you anything? Water, coffee, whiskey?"

Harper laughs. "Some water would be great. I'm really sorry for your loss, Jessa. I understand the two of you were very close."

"I still can't believe she's gone. I keep waiting to wake up, like it's a dream or something."

He follows her into the kitchen, walnut cabinets and countertops topped with Carrara marble, finished with custom-made satin nickel appliances.

Jessa is all legs, no waist, and beautiful perky tits. Harper, usually impeccably dressed in black suits, perfectly tailored to his tall frame, is suddenly self-conscious that he's wearing yesterday's clothes.

Something about this girl made him want to look his best.

Jessa focuses on her task, and this gives Harper the opportunity to watch her. He smiles at the libidinous nature of his thoughts. She looks up and doesn't freeze.

Instead, she smiles warmly, confidently.

He follows her to the living room. Her laptop is open, and a dog-eared book, *Delta of Venus*, lies on the floor, next to a pair of red-soled stilettos.

Jessa didn't look like a college kid as he watches her move with the grace and confidence of a woman.

"So, can you tell me a little bit about your relationship with Brooke?"

Harper isn't getting a sense of loss from Jessa. He can read people; this is his gift. She is drumming her finger on her leg, unable to make eye contact, as if she is nervous and afraid.

"What are you studying?"

"Medieval and Renaissance studies."

Harper thinks of Brooke's murder and the connection to the Renaissance Killer, the Deer Island murders. He remembers Belle saying that the last victim, Helena Achlys, was poisoned by Ouabain. His mind races, trying to make more of a connection. Maybe Brooke had found the killer and planned to report him on the night she was murdered.

"Medieval and Renaissance studies. What do you do with that?"

"I have no idea." Jessa laughs nervously. Her eyes travel down his body. She blushes, beet red. "Sort of an obsession of mine."

"Do you have any idea if Brooke was involved in another religion?"

"Brooke was Catholic. She went to church every Sunday," Jessa says.

She runs her hands over her black dress and curls her long legs underneath her body, sitting next to him on the fur-covered couch.

He thinks about Seraphina. The last thing he needs is another complication. He realizes this is all Jessa will be to him. So nice to see a woman in something tight, not like the shapeless dresses he is used to seeing Seraphina in.

With Jessa, he loses his train of thought. He isn't used to this. He is trained to always keep his face neutral, never react, a skill that keeps him alive in aggressive situations and is often the key in uncovering the truth.

She sighs as if tired from sorting out her emotions and says, "I met Brooke at a club. I was bartending at the time. She was new to the city. I got her a job waitressing with me. We lived together for a few months."

"Were you sleeping with her?"

"Is that relevant?"

"If it wasn't, I wouldn't ask."

"Yes. But that ended a few months ago."

"Why?"

"She met someone. The guy was really bad news. Super-controlling and possessive. She wouldn't listen to me. She was stubborn. Look what it cost her."

"Is that why you moved out?"

"That and a good couple of months at work. It was either rent my own place or go to Vegas to see if I could double it."

Their eyes lock; hers are open and fearless. Harper is fascinated and determined to stay in control. He makes sure she is the first to look away.

"Listen, I never met him. I always assumed he was married. She never said so, but that would explain all of the secrecy. The good ones always are. Like you, Harper. I'm guessing you're married."

"Yes, I am."

"What a waste," she says with a devilish smile.

"My wife doesn't think so."

"Well, if you want information, it's going to cost you." Her lashes gleam over her bright-blue eyes.

"How about I subpoena you and put your ass on the stand?"

He glares at her, hoping to intimidate. His pulse races, and he weakens. He is distracted by her lips, her legs, her perfume.

The effect she has on him is a total loss of equilibrium.

"I just meant dinner. I'm starving. Do you mind if we talk over dinner?"

Harper feels off his game tonight. He thinks about Seraphina at home with Sky. Dinner with Jessa seems like a bad idea.

Then he hears himself say, "I know a great neighborhood place."

Four

HARPER AND JESSA

They step outside into the wind and rain. Harper's cheap umbrella flips upside down, and they both laugh as he battles the wind. Finally, he gives up and tosses it in the garbage as they run. He tries to shield Jessa from the rain with his newspaper.

Both wet, they find shelter inside Boccaccio restaurant; it's warm and comfortable. The maroon-tuxedoed waiters and Motown music blaring through the monotone speakers are a relaxing vibe.

"So this is all it takes. A little penne a la vodka and you'll sing like a canary?" Harper says, trying to dry off with a napkin.

"That's right," she says, giggling.

"You want wine?"

"No, thank you."

"We'll have the Merlot, please."

"Are you always this domineering?"

"What, these are my people! I've got a lot of pull here," he says with delight, waving over another waiter, who promptly ignores him.

They both laugh. The waiter returns with the menu. "Make that a bottle of Merlot. We may be here a while," he says, looking outside at the pouring rain, an embarrassed grin spreading over his face.

There's something about Jessa. She is getting under his skin and inside his head. He has never felt a sexual attraction like this; not since Seraphina. He knows it isn't the right thing, but he wants Jessa. Every part of him wants her. Harper can tell she is nervous but trying to hide it.

The waiter cuts through the tension, setting a wine glass down in front of Harper. He swishes the wine around in his glass and then takes a sip.

"It's good, thanks."

"Harp, it's all pretty weird. The stuff with Brooke. That's why I wanted to see you and talk to you about it. I need to make sure I'm kept out of any sort of trial."

Jessa takes a sip and sets her glass down with a heavy sigh, squaring her shoulders like she did at home. The protective wall she's built goes up around her.

"What, you need to wait for your pasta? Go on," he says mockingly.

She really is the whole package: sweet, sexy, and confident. He can't take his eyes off her skyscraper heels and legs crossed elegantly. Her leg lightly touches his.

Why couldn't he have a little fun? No harm in that, is there?

"Those are beautiful shoes," he says, hoping she will relax a little.

"Louboutin. Only the best," she says, smiling and finally relaxing enough to find the words. "So one night a few months ago, Brooke came home from class really excited. She said she met someone, and—this is cheesy, but she was heavily into numerology, and he was her perfect match. Their love was written in the stars, crazy shit. He would tell her fortune and give her readings. One day, he gave her a Powerball number. She played it, and it actually hit."

"What was the number?"

"Twenty-three."

"The twenty-three enigma."

"What is that?"

"It's an occult theory that ties into the Law of Fives, based on the belief that most events are connected to the number twenty-three."

"I don't know anything about that, but she bought a flat-screen TV and new laptops."

"Go on," Harper says.

"He also gave her some sort of note written in code. She spent hours at her computer and on all those crazy Internet sleuthing websites trying to figure out the code. She skipped classes and everything. She finally figured out it was an invite to some underground party. Some secret society called the Skull Club. They meet online in chat rooms and at places all over the city to try to solve murders."

"Sort of like the Skeleton Crew," Harper says.

"Who?"

"The Skeleton Crew. They started out as amateur online detectives, hobbyists that spend countless unpaid hours trying to find missing persons and convict killers," Harper says. "I think most of them do more harm than good."

Harper remembers the case that kicked it all off back in 1998, when the Web was just getting started: "Tent Girl."

Wilbur Riddle, who had been scavenging for glass insulators alongside Route 25 in Kentucky, discovered a decomposing body of a young woman wrapped in a heavy green canvas tarpaulin.

The case went cold for thirty years until a factory worker, Todd

Matthews, matched her to a listing posted by a woman in search of her long-lost sister.

Matthews's track record of solving cases eventually led to a position as communications director for the Missing and Unidentified Persons System, or NamUs, a clearinghouse established by the Department of Justice.

"This is much darker than that. This crew isn't satisfied with just reenacting and solving the murders; they're much more interested in the finding and punishing part."

"You mean, like vigilantes?" He looks at her through slanted eyes. Harper thinks about the information from the Boston Police about the murder of Helena Achlys.

Belle's words replay in his mind: *It's a poison used for hunting and warfare. She was hunted, Harp.*

"Yes. Brooke told me the night of the murder that she tried to break up with him. It was too much. She started crying. She seemed really scared. I didn't know what to do. But when I left the party that night, she was still alive. That's really all I know."

To Harper, omission is as much a crime as lying. He hates liars. It always makes him feel like maybe he just isn't worth the truth.

The waiter sets down the food.

When Harper looks out the window, dusk has fallen and the rain has stopped. The thought of another night alone is miserable. The thought of going home is even more miserable. He leans back and runs his hands through his hair.

"So do you have any kids?" Jessa says.

"A daughter. Her name is Sky. How about you? How come you're not out with your boyfriend tonight?"

"No boyfriend. Still waiting for my Henry Miller, I guess."

Harper can't get enough of Jessa. He knows she is hiding something and that he will uncover the truth eventually.

His attraction for her is overwhelming. "Listen, maybe I should go. You know you can come by the office and we can take a statement." His frayed nerves are getting the best of him.

"But you didn't get what you came for," she says, her lips so full and beautiful. She rests her hand on his knee under the table.

"Am I going to get what I came for?" Harper says, his voice deep and labored with lust.

She doesn't fight to fill the gaps in conversation. She waits, grabbing his full attention before answering.

"I haven't decided."

She has the most beautiful hair. She ties it back, off her face, and takes off her jacket.

"But you are thinking about it." He laughs at his enthusiasm and lack of elegance.

Jessa is all sex, the promise of a chemical reaction so mind-blowing, he loses himself in the anticipation of it.

Her eyes like a mood ring, changing from the icy blue of winter to a darker slate gray, the color of the sky in the pouring rain. Her black dress hugs every curve.

He checks his phone and realizes he has several texts from Belle and a few from Seraphina.

ARE YOU EVER COMING HOME?

He has gone off the grid, and it feels good.

He sends Seraphina a text, letting her know that he will be home late.

Just a little longer, he thinks to himself as he shuts down the phone.

"How about you, Harper? How did you become one of the good guys?"

Harper takes a deep breath. "Is that what you think I am? One of the good guys?"

"I'm optimistic, so far."

"Well, I guess I always wanted to be a hero. My old man was a drunk, which didn't really excuse him for being a major asshole. He drank every paycheck on his way out the door."

"That's sad."

"Not really. In a way, he motivated me. I didn't have to spend my life trying to be like him. I think it was Harvey Dent who said: 'You either die a hero, or you live long enough to see yourself become the villain.' I'm not sure what that has to do with anything. I better stop drinking," he says with an amused expression.

She watches him intently with those big blue eyes. He's uncomfortable with the depth of her gaze. Harper has always been able to get people talking. But with Jessa, it is so easy to be naked.

"Listen, I'm not sure what we are doing here," Harper says, shifting uncomfortably in his seat.

"We're just talking. It seems like you needed someone to listen tonight. So let me do that for you." She laughs. "It's the least I can do, really. Before you go back to saving the world."

This girl. Is she reading my mind?

"Excuse me. I'm just going to run to the ladies' room before we go."

He watches her move with the grace of a dancer, and so does every other man at the bar.

While he's contemplating what to do, his phone starts vibrating in his pocket. It's Belle. Against his better judgment, he turns it off altogether.

Jessa reappears, and in a room full of art, he has eyes only for her. Eyes meet; honest and open, she is searching for something.

"What's wrong?" Harper asks.

"I'm an idiot. I lost an earring."

"Here?"

"No, earlier. At my apartment. It went right down the drain in my bathroom. It was one of the ones my grandmother gave me. The super still hasn't called me back."

"You just have to open up the drain. It's easy."

"Do I look like a girl who knows how to just open up the drain?"

"Not really. Listen, let's get the check. I'll do it for you, and then I'll head out."

"Are you sure, really? That would be amazing. Thank you so much."

Harper helps Jessa with her coat. She trips on her way out the door and falls back against him. Her scent is intoxicating, like flowers and expensive perfume. He breathes in and is under her spell.

She unlocks the elevator and they step in.

Harper can feel his heartbeat quicken, his fingers aching to touch her. She brushes her body against him and catches her breath, biting her lip seductively.

"Are you sure, Jessa?"

"Ask me again, Harp, and I just might change my mind." She takes her key out of the elevator, locking it between floors.

"Jessa," he says, his voice sounding distant. Her hands are all over his body.

He caresses her lips; the feel of her skin is delicate, like silk. She presses hard against the taut muscles of his chest. Her fingers dance lightly down his shoulders. She feels the bulge of his gun around his waist.

He's lost in her, aroused by her caresses. He takes her hair down; so sexy, loose and disheveled. Her dress falls off her shoulders, leaving her breasts exposed.

His lips run down her neck. She moans, her senses in overdrive.

Her submission makes him desire her even more. His needs fill up the space between them.

He needs to explore her, devour her.

She teases, biting down on his lip playfully. Her cheeks flush with desire. She reaches into her handbag; it spills all over the floor. She finds the condom she is looking for, and she stares at him searchingly.

"You must have been such a good Girl Scout."

He unzips her dress, and it drops to floor. She is naked, breasts exposed and nipples hard and pink.

He kisses her lips, moving down her chin, tracing her toned stomach with his fingers. His hands move down, through the lace of her panties; she is wet with desire.

He can't take his eyes off her as she pulls down the zipper of his pants.

He lifts her up and pushes her roughly against the wall, pinning her arms above her head. Legs around his back, locking behind, she moans in ecstasy as his fingers explore her.

"Now," she whispers and drags her fingers through his dark hair.

Her eyes challenge him, so wide open. She is at his mercy. He likes the feeling of power. She is all lust and passion, gyrating, her body a vibration of heat and electricity. She arches her back into him, deeper, his hands gripping, orgasms building, all hips and thighs until they are over the edge and climaxing in each other's arms.

She screams as if she were at the top of a roller coaster. Jessa is unusually beautiful, her features almost Egyptian, red hair and sapphire eyes—smoldering and sweet. He buries his head in her hair, detecting the smell of sandalwood, as she covers him with butterfly kisses.

He would reenact the scene over and over in his mind: her dress slipping off her shoulder, their legs coiled, his desire ready to strike.

He hears a strange, muffled banging. It takes a minute for Harper to realize it's coming from outside, and not just the pounding of his heart inside his chest.

"Hey, let the elevator go!" The words are followed by more angry shouting. They both laugh and scramble to dress and pick up the contents of Jessa's purse.

Once together, he turns the key, and the elevator lurches into motion, opening up into her apartment.

Harper smiles and pulls her close. He whispers, "Let me guess, Jessa. That whole story about the earring—you made it all up, didn't you?"

"Please don't be angry."

He moves closer to her, skimming his fingertips across her cheek, and kisses her passionately.

"Jessa, I'm married, and I'm not going to leave my wife."

She wraps her arms around his waist and presses her body against his.

"I know. You'll see. I can be very discreet." Above her, written in neon blue lights, the glow of modern art that reads, YOU ARE HERE.

He walks through the dark streets of SoHo toward where he parked the car. He is starting to feel like Seraphina, the gears in his mind always shifting and moving, body on overdrive.

The same thought keeps turning over in his mind, so he says it out loud: "Fuck, what have I done?"

He puts the key in the ignition and pulls out onto the road. The tires crunch and the engine hums as he pulls onto the West Side Highway. He is driving too fast, in and out of the lanes.

His trousers are wrinkled, and his shirt needs pressing, but that's to be expected after a night with Jessa. She is a natural beauty with her shiny red hair and that killer body. And the sex, that alone is scandalous.

Now he is a cheater, and nothing else matters. That one choice invalidated all of the other good he has tried to do.

He is angry—angry at Seraphina for all of her weakness. All of it, her fault.

She brought him down just like she always threatened to do. She had always been consumed by darkness. He thought he could save her, but no, she had to take him with her. So fucking selfish. Well, he wouldn't let her. He would fight it.

She isn't sick, just needy; another spoiled rich girl who will do anything to get her way. He pulls onto the Garden State and sees a car pulled over on the side of the road. He breathes in deeply and forces himself to slow down.

He calls Belle.

"Where the hell have you been?"

"With Jessa."

"You mean Jessica."

"What?"

"She's an escort, Harp. A very high-paid one at that. I'm talking two thousand an hour. She and Brooke worked together. That's why I've been trying to reach you. Check your e-mail."

Harper recounts his conversation with her. He can't believe it. He had been involved with the agency bust of Jay Eckler, Metropolitan Confidential, a guy who filled his days shopping for jewelry at Cartier in SoHo or shoe shopping for his girls at Manolo Blahnik.

At night, he would be at Cipriani with a bottle of Johnnie Walker Blue, handing out his signature titanium business cards. The type of guy Harper loved to destroy.

"What agency?"

"These girls are on their own. They meet clients online and carefully vet them. It's a tight network. A girls' club. She had some very powerful clients, ones that have a lot to lose if word of any of this gets out," Belle says. "We don't have any other names, and we're looking for the guy who handles their books. The story is going to break tomorrow. I told them to keep Jessa's name out of the news for now. She's the only lead we've got. You still there, Harp?"

"Yeah, thanks. I'm pulling into the driveway. Nice job. We'll catch up in the morning."

He pulls over to the side of the road and just sits in silence, thinking it over.

He opens an e-mail from Belle and clicks on the hyperlink. It's an image of Jessa, dressed in a tight black lace dress, superimposed against the glowing lights of Manhattan after dark.

The next picture, she's in black lace, red lips, and sky-high heels, and one word: *luxury*.

He clicks on it, blood pressure rising. Another link; *Indulge me*.

The rain has turned to ice and snow; it whips and whirls outside his window.

"Jessica." He lets the name roll off his tongue.

He doesn't like the sound of it, not one little bit.

Five

LARA KANE

Most autopsies are standard. After an external examination, Y- and U-shaped incisions are made, and the organs are removed, weighed, and inspected. In this case, the bloating in the abdominal area from bacteria and gases caused putrefaction.

Harper had sent someone from his office to oversee the autopsy. So instead of getting a call from the medical examiner, Chief Assistant DA Lara Kane is waiting for him in his office. She is young and hungry, a graduate of Brown who recently joined the team.

Harper waves her in.

She sneezes and wipes her nose as she steps into the room. "It's a good thing I don't mind cleaning up messes, Harp."

"Women's work," he says, smiling.

Lara responds to his misogynistic quip with a flip of her middle finger.

"Enlighten me."

"I think I just did," she says.

SEEING RED

Now he's laughing out loud. "Are you feeling all right?" Harper has a way with women. He can charm anyone, even the staunchest feminist, like Lara.

"Just a cold," Lara says with no emotion or affection, leading him to believe he is failing to charm her. He will have to change that.

Belle walks in. "I'll brief Harper, Lara. Can you grab the photographs?"

Lara shoots Harper a look and walks out. "Did I piss her off again?" Harper asks.

"She was headed that way when she got in. But you didn't help matters much."

"Is that the autopsy report?"

"Brooke had contusions and abrasions of the scalp. Her fractures are complex, showing a lot of force. All the slash wounds were made by a single-edged knife about six inches long. It takes skill to remove those organs with such speed and precision. Whoever did this has most likely done it before."

"Why do you say that?"

"I've seen calves butchered, and I can tell by the clean lines and the cutting around the organs that the man who did this has done it before."

Harper doesn't want to hear this. Belle is hinting at the possibility of a serial killer.

"He has knowledge of police procedures and forensics; this is not your average thrill-seeking psychopath. He may have used chloroform or trichloromethane to knock out his victim."

Harper realizes this makes perfect sense. Chloroform is a sweet-smelling, colorless liquid that can be vaporized into a gas to numb the pain. It was first used as an anesthetic in 1847 by a Scottish obstetrician,

James Young Simpson, who tried it out on two of his dinner party guests, purely for entertainment purposes."

"So Brooke Beck was still alive when they started cutting," Belle says.

Harper nods solemnly. "That would explain why she didn't put up a fight, and nobody heard any screaming. Did anything show up in the tox report?"

"No, but that doesn't mean much. Chloroform has a very high evaporation rate, although it can leave traces of burning on the skin if it comes in contact with the nose or mouth of the victim. Brooke didn't have any of that."

"This guy is a pro. Maybe he has some military training. He's fast, efficient and a skilled surgeon," Harper says.

"During the Civil War, ether and chloroform became indispensable tools for military doctors, who performed tens of thousands of amputations on the battlefield."

Lara returns with a steaming cup of coffee and the crime scene photos.

She does a double take, looking at Harper now with a mischievous gleam in her eyes, the same one she gets before she is about to deliver another lame-brained gibe.

"Are you wearing the same clothes as yesterday?" Lara takes out her phone and points it at him. She takes a picture.

"What are you planning to do with that?" he asks.

"Well, this is such a stretch from your compulsive metrosexual nature. Maybe I'll post it on Facebook. Then I'll tweet it and put it up on Instagram. So, not much."

"I had a fight with my wife, so I slept here last night. Feel bad now?"

"You fight a lot."

"Is that a question?"

"More of an observation."

"Yes. Seraphina and I fight. We're married. That's what married people do. Listen, when it comes to my marriage, why don't you leave the detective work to me."

"Sure," Lara says, burying her eyes in the paperwork, realizing she struck a nerve. "We got the results back from the forensic botanist."

Lara takes out the evidence bag containing the brown bean from the crime scene and says, "The Calabar bean is a plant indigenous to the coastal area of southeastern Nigeria known as Calabar. The seed is extremely poisonous, and it's extracted from the Calabar bean, scientifically known as *Physostigma venenosum*. The effects are similar to that of nerve gases used in war; they disrupt communication between muscles and the nervous system. It's got quite a history. African tribes called it the 'ordeal bean.'"

"What is an ordeal bean?" Harper says with a short, nervous laugh.

"West African tribes used it as a system of law, by feeding a few seeds to the accused and subjecting them to a dangerous experience or 'trial by ordeal.'

"They believed God would perform a miracle and let the accused live if they were innocent. If not, they died from the poison, and justice would be served."

"That's some nut," Harper says. Belle starts to laugh.

"If you swallow the bean whole, you have a better chance of surviving," Lara says, ignoring their frat-boy behavior. "They used the power of the beans to detect witches and people possessed by evil spirits."

Belle shows Harper his notebook, where he has drawn a picture of a bean and written, "This is nuts!"

"And one last thing, Harp. Brooke Beck was pregnant," Lara says.

"Jesus Christ. Really?" Belle says, horrified. "That's the motive.

He knocked her up and didn't want any part of being a father, so he murders her and makes it look like a ritualistic crime."

The door bursts open, and Harper's assistant sheepishly walks in, placing the *New York Post* on his desk. The headline reads, NYU STUDENT MURDERED AND MUTILATED.

"Cindy Adams called. Again."

"Did you get a new assistant?" asks Lara.

"I didn't notice," Harper says distractedly.

"You didn't really just say that."

"I did. This office is a revolving door, and that's how we roll."

She rolls her eyes.

"And that's how I roll."

"You're pretty funny ... for a girl."

"Are those the glamour shots?" Harper says.

He takes the crime scene photographs and looks them over. "It's a shame. She was such a beautiful girl," Harper says.

"So if she were ugly, it would be okay that she was brutally murdered and dismembered?" Lara says.

Harper shoots Belle a look.

"Thanks, Lara. You can go. Feel better. Go home and get some rest."

Harper takes it all in, perplexed. This case defies Locard's Principle, a theory by Edmond Locard, also known as the Sherlock Holmes of France. He came up with the principle that every contact by a criminal leaves a trace. These traces can come in any form: a glass that shatters, fingerprints, or fibers from the clothes the killer was wearing. All of these things will serve as silent witness to the crime. In this case, so few fragments of evidence were left behind, aside from the body of the girl.

Harper hated failure of any kind. A failure to find physical evidence would weigh on him. He had always been driven by his belief in a moral and ethical universe. Yet lately, he was questioning everything.

A perfect killer is an animal at best, nothing proud or noble; all hubris and blind narcissistic rage. No added value to the human experience.

In the case of Brooke, the killer is cold and calculating. Most likely smart and psychopathic, well blended into society. Everyman. The hardest type to identify and capture. They are usually highly intelligent, methodical, and organized to the point of being meticulous.

Every detail of the crime is planned out in advance, and the killer takes precaution to make sure they leave no incriminating evidence.

They have elaborate schemes to draw the victims in and gain sympathy, taking great pride in what they consider to be their "work," paying close attention to news stories about their deeds.

Given the lack of evidence, it had to be someone who knows how to navigate the system. It could even be a detective, one who didn't put much faith in religion. Someone who had been repeatedly abused by the ones he loved most. Until one day, the only way he can find freedom is through hate, intolerance, and violence.

To the organized killer, it's all part of the game, a game that thrives on dominance and fear.

Harper looks up from the photographs at Belle. "Seraphina and I had another fight. I can't take it anymore, man."

"That's marriage, and that's why I'm single."

"Is this marriage or just my marriage? She's paranoid, Belle. She thinks someone is stalking her. The nightmares are getting worse. She won't talk to me. She won't see a doctor. She says she saw a boat off our dock and someone is stalking her. She needs help or medication, something. It's getting to the point where I'm afraid to leave her alone with the baby."

"Harp, you love Seraphina. You have a good marriage. You're still fighting to change each other. It's when you stop that you've got a real problem. She's strong-willed and passionate, maybe a little crazy. You just need to spend more time with her. You look like hell. You need to take a vacation. You can't keep burning the candle."

Harper says, "I was up all night reading the threads on those Internet detective websites. You were right. All of our personal information about the night Seraphina was attacked is out there. They're picking through clues, examining every piece of data, like vultures. Why can't they leave the past alone?"

Harper didn't plan on going off. He planned on keeping his mouth shut and doing his job like every other day. He says, "I've dedicated my life to fighting crime from the front lines. I'm in the trenches, day after day.

"Truthfully, I wish I was there and that I killed him. Nobody has the right to do that to a woman. Seraphina can't remember anything from that night. It is hard to imagine that she could defend herself and have killed the man that attacked her. We need to look into the Renaissance Killer and pull up anything that might give us a clue about Brooke Beck's murder. Seraphina thinks it's all connected, and the picture hanging above Brooke's bed is one of the few clues we have to go on."

Other than Seraphina, Belle is the only one who truly knows him, the depth of his pain and anger.

Harper wrestles with the demons from his past. He never had much of a childhood. Harper's father had no compass for his soul. He was an abusive alcoholic, the memories an albatross Harper carries with him in the recesses of his mind.

Harper took care of his mother, financially and even physically, until she passed away when he was in high school. She was always sick and depressed. He couldn't save her from the damage his father had inflicted. The pain of Seraphina and her illness brings him back to that time with his mother, and he can't face it again. He feels like he's going off the rails and Belle is the only one who can bring him back.

Belle says, "Each man acts on his own perception, not universal truth, so to put punishment into the hands of the people can easily lead to an abuse of power."

Harper nods. "Yes." He carries with him a deep hatred of vigilantism.

"Remember John Locke, who believed that human nature is characterized by reason and tolerance? The social contract Locke created, stating that if a government upholds the laws and protects its people, the citizens will obey the law."

Harper finishes his thought. "But when a government fails to protect, it's no longer recognized, and punishment can fall into the wrong hands, the hands of the people."

Harper is still feeling the anger coursing through him, the darkness of his secrets threatening to take him under.

"If left unchecked, we become a dangerous group of vigilantes and a society that can't remain free," Belle says. "That's why we wake up every day. That's why we get out of bed in the morning and come to work. And I'm always here to remind you."

Belle's words numb Harper's expectations like a drug. The light streams in through the skylight. Harper breathes and makes the choice to let the light in.

Six

SERAPHINA AND HARPER

Under pressure, things can break. Show me all of the scars you hide. My mirrored heart is made of glass. Once shattered, it's gone forever. I will always be the fool who rushes in, but for Harper, love is only his reflection.

I watch Sky play in her crib quietly when the text comes in. I can feel the phone vibrate, and I know it's bad news even before I look. I know I will be angry. I promise myself I will not, but even before I look, a part of me knows I have lost.

DON'T WAIT UP. LOVE, HARP

I think he has this text on auto-send. He's been home late every night this week.

I send a simple smiley-face emoji because my phone does not have two smiley face emojis, one with hands wrapped around the other and beating its tiny, happy head against a brick wall.

I can feel the heat of my anger and frustration rise into my cheeks. Sky starts to cry, as if she can feel my pain.

"It's not your fault, sweet baby."

Our love, a love that cuts like a diamond. Stone against stone. Unbreakable. A love that fills you up and takes your breath away.

I check my voicemail. It's the guy from the security company. I picked it for the name, B-Protected. I didn't check the reviews on Yelp. I just picked up the phone and dialed.

"We're not going to make it today. This job is going to take another day or so; we'll have to reschedule."

My impulsivity is another thing that drives Harper crazy. He used to love it, but that was when it involved sex in his office after hours. Apparently not so much when you're impulse buying off Net-a-Porter at five in the morning, trolling for deals. After all, a girl can't be too hard driving when it comes to having a virtual edge in fashion.

I triple lock the doors and go through my ritual, closing the shades, locking out the monsters that live mostly in my mind. The rest of my world has gone black and white, but with Harper, it's frozen in shades of gray.

I go to Sky. She is standing, smiling, wide-eyed, as I take her from Birdie.

"You can go now, Birdie. I'll see you tomorrow."

"Ms. Sera, they installed the cameras today. They said they'd be back in the morning to show you the new alarm."

"I thought they canceled. Harp must have set it up." I think to myself, *At least he's good for something.*

I sit down on the rocker and open my shirt, and Sky drinks the last bit of milk from my breast without taking her eyes off of me.

"Hi, sweet baby," I whisper softly. She puts her tiny hand in mine.

We rock, and I soothe, holding on like it's the end of the world. There's no peace like the one that comes from holding this child close, giving her my full love and attention.

"Such small hands, Sky, but they are gonna do big things," I say, kissing her delicate fingers.

For a minute, it's us against the world. Not just me, lost, banging my head against a steel drum.

Sky tucks herself into me and falls asleep. So happy, so content.

I put her back down to sleep. She will be up for her last feed around midnight. I pump the rest of the milk and put it in the refrigerator. The next batch will be toxic, riddled with alcohol.

I'll have to pump and dump as I've done every night this week.

I think about Harper's words when we first moved to the suburbs. "We made this choice together," he would say. "So your unhappiness, Seraphina, is on you. Don't blame me."

He's not wrong. I reluctantly agreed to leave New York City when the baby was born. Harper wanted more space and a house on the water.

It's hard to be modest in a city like New York that's home to eight million people. You have to be willing to share not just your space but your life experiences.

That's what I miss most, the feeling of being connected to other people. It made me feel safe when most nights I felt as if there was nothing keeping my thoughts from spinning me right off the planet.

Now I spend most nights alone and searching for peace at the bottom of a bottle.

Harper could count on me to always draw blood and scratch at the surface of things until I exposed the brutal, raw truth.

That's what Harper was like in the courtroom. That's what we have in common.

I take another pill, and against my better judgment, I search his gym bag. He's out late every night and doesn't answer my texts. Harper is lying. I can feel it. I need proof. Otherwise, he will only accuse me of being paranoid and anxious. With all of my drinking and the pills, he isn't far from the truth. I wanted justice. I needed to know the truth. I'm alone every night, and he has his freedom.

At the bottom of his gym bag, all balled up, I find a hotel receipt for the Greenwich Hotel. I check the date on my calendar. I was home with Sky. I hate him now; and then, I love him so completely, it's like whiplash.

I take another pill to get me through another long night alone. The memory of our passion, the life we've built together, keeps me here like glue, so fragile now, held together with sticks and string.

The doorbell rings, jolting me from my thoughts. My anxiety is on the rise. It rings again, waking up Sky. I take her downstairs and look out the glass pane to see a stranger.

Sky is crying, sensing my fear, and I realize I forgot to button my shirt from breastfeeding. I scramble to cover myself.

"Ms. Swift?"

"Yes. And it's Mrs. Swift. My husband is just upstairs."

Something about him is strange and awkward. I feel threatened. The estate is too quiet, making me feel very alone.

My eyes dart around outside.

I can hear a dog barking in the distance. Aside from that, nothing.

The quiet of the suburbs brings me no peace.

"I installed your digital security system."

Sky looks up at me for reassurance. I didn't hear his name or any words that came after.

I couldn't take my eyes off the boat slowly cutting through the water.

It is a dark, starless night. I can see the boat stop just a few miles off our dock. The trees sway in the yard, but there is no breeze. I can feel his eyes on me.

"Let's get you set up," he says with a strange smile. My shirt now buttoned, the feeling of his gaze still burns into me. I bring Sky up closer to my chest for comfort.

"Just punch a four-digit code in for me, please."

"Okay." I put in the digits of Sky's date of birth.

"You're all set. Just don't forget it," he says, laughing as if I'm a moron.

"Just in time," he says.

"What do you mean?"

"You didn't hear about the break-in up on Navesink Road, further down the river? Some sort of home invasion. They got beat up pretty badly."

A break-in? My mind twists. I have to call Harper. He's getting closer. We have to do something.

"Just kidding, shit like that doesn't happen in fancy neighborhoods like this," he says in a patronizing tone.

"Thanks. I've got the code, and I'm pretty sure I can take it from here."

I start to shut the door. He stops me.

"I just need your e-mail, so I can send you the link to access the video on your phone."

"Sure."

He hands me a pen, and I write it down for him. He leans in closer. He has jet-black hair and smells like a mix of hair dye and cigarettes. "Now you be careful," he says with a sneer, as if I am protecting my home from him. His hand goes to his forehead in a mocking salute.

I close my eyes, concentrate, and focus on staying calm.

My phone buzzes with a text.

You can't hit a target with your eyes closed.

My heart beats faster. Someone is playing games with me. Harper is keeping me at arm's length; he isn't protecting us.

My head is spinning, and when I look down, the text vanishes before I can get a screen shot of it as proof. I'm questioning whether any of this is real. It's my marriage, this house in the suburbs, Harper's lies that make me question my own sanity. He's making me crazy; the anxiety rises and fills me up like a balloon, carrying me away from my life. If I'm not careful, I will end up insane. He'll have me medicated and locked up. He will throw away the key, taking me further from Sky. Harper can never give her the love and affection she needs.

These thoughts are quickly replaced with my own needs. Tonight it's a perfectly chilled, spicy Bloody Mary.

I push closed all of the windows. I glance back out, and I can see the security van is gone from the driveway.

The storm clouds have moved in over the dock, swallowing up the stars in the sky.

I can feel someone watching me. I can see his shadowy form standing on the deck of the boat. A heavy rain is starting to fall. The boat is old, with dull white paint. The drops of rain bounce off the water. I can't take my eyes off of him.

He must be soaked. The rain beats down on him, but he doesn't move. I can feel the hair on my arms prickle and the anger race through me.

Who stands outside in weather like this?

Is anyone out there, or is it just my imagination?

A few seconds later, my phone buzzes from the pocket of my jeans. The screen reads Blocked Number.

"Hello?" I say, with a voice faint as a whisper. But I get no response.

"Hello? Is someone there?"

I can hear someone breathing on the other end of the line, but I still get no response.

"Leave us alone!" I scream and throw the phone to the ground.

I pry myself from the window. I tell myself it's just my imagination and that someone isn't getting off on making me uncomfortable.

My teeth are chattering, and my whole body is shaking.

I remind myself I have an alarm now. We are safe. This is just my imagination playing tricks. Sky has drifted off peacefully to sleep.

Always treat the side effects until you get to the root of the illness. That's how I justify my drinking. I'm still digging, just kicking at the roots.

I'm horrible. I know. Harper is right. I'm drinking too much. I just can't face another night alone, rattling around in the shadows of my memories. I can't seem to stop piling rocks on my marriage, one by one. Pretty soon we will all be buried under the weight of my insanity.

I've watched Harper drift farther and farther away from me, and now we are lost in a sea of my delusion and irrationality.

Since the birth of our child, everything has become about everyone else; my happiness and pain, an afterthought. Now Harper sparkles and glows while I suffer. I can picture him out tonight with a beautiful new girl by his side.

My marriage is falling apart, and when night falls, we always manage to crawl back behind the lines. During the day it's an all-out war, a barrage of texting and e-mails fired like bullets from a gun.

I have no one to call for advice.

I was born and raised in Miami, a backdrop of broken beauty somehow stifled by the stunted seasons. I was beyond privileged, with a car and driver at my disposal and every freedom that came with wealth and power.

My father liked his women diagnosed and medicated, and that

was the case with my mother most of the time. She wanted no part of being a mother.

For her, a child was for show, one more notch toward having it all, but secretly a threat, each year chipping away at her fragile illusion of youth and beauty.

My father, famed plastic surgeon Dr. Michael Whitlock, was the author of the Pulitzer Prize-winning *My Pretty Mommy*, a novel that explains the need for plastics at every phase of motherhood. They are a match made in heaven. Neither can be bothered to fix anything under the hood; nothing matters more than the superficial quest for perfection, beauty, money, power, and eternal youth.

Sadly, after I was attacked, "ugly, bloody, and broken" were all words I would use to describe the new me.

Although they tried, it was just too painful for my parents to process. They asked me to put my secrets in a little box, forget they ever happened, and move forward with a smile.

Even with my father's magic with a needle and thread, I look in the mirror now, and all I see are scars.

All the king's horses and all the king's men couldn't put Seraphina back together again.

He didn't want me to talk about it. He was embarrassed. He just gave me pills that made me numb and able to move forward.

My childhood memories are disconnected and broken. Mostly, I can remember my parents fighting, voices loud as thunder, like smoke through a chimney, rising up into my bedroom at night, suffocating me in my bed.

My mother was never satisfied. She always wanted more—more money, more beauty, more love, even though her superficial beauty was nothing more than a lucky accident. Too often, I was left alone with my own darkness when I was hurt. So now, in order to survive, I stay away from the relationships I need most.

I live a life of detachment, and I only feel free when I'm painting. The colors on canvas give me life and fill in the broken pieces of me that are dull and gray. With the passing of my childhood, a new door opened, and with it, I got stronger.

I left my family behind, at least the darkness of it, and moved into a better place, one of hope and promise.

Sky coos sweetly, and the monitor brings me back to the present. The rain has stopped, and the water is smooth like glass. The boat is gone, and I wonder if it was nothing more than an illusion or a side effect of the growing madness within me.

I walk out into the crisp night air. I feel like I'm breaking from all the stress. The second drink. Always liquid courage.

The chill feels good as I walk across the grounds of Seablades and out onto the dock.

I will put together the broken pieces, and those places will heal stronger than before.

I make my way across the grass barefoot and enter the art studio. I can feel my fear cutting through the darkness. I take out a blank canvas, determined to start over. I start with red. Deep and crimson, flames thick, rising up from the bottom, death fire and combustion.

Next blue, her beautiful naked body rising up out of the flames. The lines of it, soft and sensual.

Gray. Breasts, full and swollen. Black, an arm raised, a declaration of war. Green, a tempest, storm clouds growing in the space where a child should be.

Finally, at the top of the canvas, drenched in liquid gold, I paint the head of a phoenix surrounded by sunlight.

I feel the heat of the sun as it rises, carved out of fire.

SEEING RED

The colors exploding and vibrant, this painting is beautiful and masterful, even if dark and fragmented.

With it, something of recognition, of memory, seems to awaken within me.

I step back to admire my work, and in the distance I see a silhouette out on the dock. For a moment, my levity dies, and the irrational fears take over.

I am frozen. A stranger is watching me, a shadow, swaying in the darkness of the night. I reach for my cell and start to dial 911. When he turns, I can see the glowing embers of Harper's cigarette.

Through the darkness, our eyes meet.

I make my way outside, heart still racing from the adrenaline and alcohol.

"What are you doing up so late?" he asks.

"Painting. You're smoking again?"

He laughs as if this is the least of our problems—and he is right.

He studies my face, my eyes, my body as if I'm someone he's just met in a smoky bar or had a one-night stand with and wants to leave but doesn't quite know how to say it.

I move in closer, angling in toward his neck.

He smells like perfume, and not mine. Some expensive brand that I don't even recognize.

He is caught off guard. I take a deeper breath in.

I try to endure my rage so I don't get consumed by it, swallowed up into the abyss of this black hole.

But it gets the best of me, and I lean into it, biting down hard into his neck and drawing blood.

"What the fuck?" he says, retreating in pain.

What have you done, Harper? I think as I walk away. *And what have we done to each other?*

Seven
SERAPHINA AND CARTER

I have no idea where my husband slept last night. I only know it wasn't with me. I never sleep anymore. I'm an insomniac. My mind isn't at peace, my eyes burning as if they are full of dust and ash.

Sleep is always a battle, a war I can't win. I feel myself ripping at the seams, just a little at a time.

Stars can live several billion years, the core expanding, cooling, and changing. They are born, they live, and then die, sometimes exploding into a supernova.

When I first met Harper, it was as if the fates had aligned, our love born out of tragedy and maelstrom. The stars were bringing us together; all heat, light, and electricity. Now I know nothing lasts forever.

I'm on the 8:40 train into Penn Station this morning. It's a fast train, and it feels like I'm really going somewhere, even though it's only to see Dr. Gordon Ellis.

I'm going because I have no filter for my words and emotions anymore. They pour out of me, polluting the fresh air around me.

I'm sitting in an aisle seat, because I'm the last one onto the train. I'm late for everything. I like the aisle seat because I always have to go to the bathroom, and I hate having to squeeze by. Now, I already have to go. The air is stale, a mixture of morning breath and coffee.

I walk down the tight aisle, the tracks shift, and I knock into a man's elbow on the way. He shoots me a look of daggers as if it were on purpose.

I shut the door behind me and click the lock into place. Train bathrooms make me think of the mother who gave birth on a moving train in India. A newborn baby fell right out and into the toilet. The infant was dubbed a "miracle baby" after she survived falling through the lavatory system and clattering onto the tracks.

It's hard to imagine, right out of the womb, such an unspeakable horror. Another little girl who will learn the language of pain before she even takes her first breath. I can almost hear the sound of my heart breaking.

I make my way back through the car and find my seat. As I walk, I hear a voice calling my name. "Seraphina?"

I turn to see Carter James Nikol, the best thing about my Eastern and Western Approach to Medicine lecture at Harvard.

"I thought that was you. You walked right by me. You haven't changed a bit," he says.

He is handsome and charismatic. Carter's still-young face is framed by dark hair, and his eyes hold the same intensity. He brightens with a smile as he looks at me.

"Do you live in the city now?" I ask.

"Mostly out in Montauk, but I have a place in the city. I still teach a few nights a week. How about you? Are you still painting?"

"I just started again, actually."

The train has pulled into his stop.

"It's great to see you, Carter."

"Listen, can we get together sometime? Maybe grab a drink?" He hands me his business card and phone number. "Really great to see you, Seraphina."

He gazes at me as if he is having trouble tearing himself away. It's almost as if I had stepped out of the frame of a portrait and he is mesmerized by the details.

I look out at the trees—pine, birch, and black locust; the gnarled ones look like devil trees. In the winter, the branches crept and tangled like a cobweb.

I think it was around this time when I first met Carter, my freshman year. I remember, it was the week before finals, and I was in my dorm room studying. The setting sun tinted the ice, and the Charles River stood still and frozen.

My roommate barged in and said, "Get your coat. We're going to see Carter James Nikol."

"Who? I'm going to the gym," I said.

"He's brilliant and life-altering, trained as a doctor and a chemist, even a mystic. He just got back from India and Nepal. He's going to lecture on fusing Eastern practice and Western medicine."

I remember I turned over in my bed and pulled the covers up.

"And he's gorgeous."

That was what woke me up and got me out of bed.

"We're going over to Countway Library. Just come with us."

When I got to the lecture, Carter was hot with an electricity that charged the room. He had a thick mop of unruly copper-colored hair, laced with silver on the sides. His thick brow, aquiline nose, and intense deep-set brown eyes scanned the crowd shrewdly behind his gray-smoke vintage eyeglasses. He was wearing a fancy Italian suit that had a sheen to it as it caught the light and a striped silk tie that added depth to the color of his eyes.

When he started talking, it was as if I was the only person in the room, instead of a lecture hall filled with hundreds of students.

I can still remember how the lecture started. Carter said, "Medicine has existed for thousands of years. During that time, most of it was an art and frequently one connected to religious or philosophical beliefs of the environment or local culture."

Carter's words lit the room on fire. "What would you do in a world without Facebook or Twitter and only a few manmade things? Anyone?"

I raised my hand.

"You pull from your environment," I said.

"That's right. The environment and your imagination."

"Any sufficiently advanced technology is indistinguishable from magic. Anybody know who said that? See me after the lecture for extra credit," Carter said.

I raised my hand again. "Arthur C. Clarke."

"That's right. What's your name?"

"Seraphina," I answered.

"Arthur C. Clarke, Isaac Asimov, and Robert Heinlein are known as the 'big three' of science fiction. Can you join me up here in front and bring your purse. I need to borrow some money."

Everyone laughed. I was enjoying all of the attention. I felt smart and funny for the first time.

Carter said, "Can I borrow a quarter, Seraphina?"

"Shouldn't I be borrowing from you? Who's the student here?" I asked innocently.

"Come on up, Seraphina. You can trust me."

I made my way toward him, feeling the heat from his stare. I handed him a quarter from my purse.

"What happens to metal when you heat it up?"

"You change the consistency of it," I said.

He took the quarter and held it tightly in his hand. "Seraphina, can you count to ten," Carter said.

As I counted, he took the quarter and bit it in half.

The students applauded and laughed.

Carter said, "That's right. Now many of you have seen this trick before. We call it magic, but I'm not a magician or a sorcerer. It's just an illusion or a manipulation of consciousness, one that can easily be explained by the powers of science."

Another student raised a hand.

"Like a drug trial, when the patient is given a placebo and fully recovers."

"That's right," Carter said, never taking his eyes off of me.

We were drawn to each other; our chemistry was palpable. Every moment with Carter had aroused in me the same curiosity and desire one feels before the curtain goes up at the theater, a rush of excitement and hope, a new world to fantasize about.

Our sexual life together had to be kept a secret. He was reactive to my moods and treated me like a moody artist and a complicated woman. He respected my painting, even encouraged it. He worshipped my body. That semester, I read avidly.

It was as if he put a spell on me and I was eager to please him.

I didn't mind his possession of me, body and soul. He shared his past and the depths of his sorrow over the loss of his mother after a long battle with depression.

Carter was born knowing how to be rich. It's not something anyone can teach you, and he knew how to use money and power to get anything he wanted.

After his family fled Nazi Germany and settled in Tulsa, Oklahoma, where his grandfather founded Nikol Oil, his father inherited control of it, and he made the most out of his wealth.

He struggled with his mother and her strict belief in Christian morality. She committed suicide after a long battle with depression.

He inherited his father's wealth and began misbehaving in school. It was rare that a family fortune survived three generations, and in this case, it was true.

After graduation from Harvard School of Medicine, he decided to travel and teach. He wrote all of his letters on an old Underwood portable typewriter that his father had given him.

A few months later, I ended things; our romance, a frenzy of love and lust, fizzled out as only a college love can do. It ended in a blaze of fireworks and unrequited glory.

After the night I was attacked, it was Carter who was by my side at the hospital, mending the parts that were broken and healing my wounds.

Harper had a bitter rivalry with Carter long before I came into the picture. Harper didn't attend a prestigious prep school like most of his peers. He worked hard to get into Harvard and attended on scholarship. He was born with luck, talent, and charisma, and had earned every penny through sweat and tears. He hated Carter for his family money and how easily life laid itself out for him. For that, the hate between them only grew, like a tree whose roots are drenched in poison.

A clash of social classes pitted them against each other, only strengthened by my brief and insignificant romance with Carter.

We arrive in Penn Station minutes later, spilling out onto the platform, up the stairs, and out onto Seventh Avenue. It's a bright and sunny day in the city.

The cirrus clouds are wispy, hanging over a tangle of dark branches in a wintery Central Park. I hail a taxi.

"Central Park West and Sixty-Eighth Street, please."

Now I'm waiting in a small room, beige on beige, with a brown door on either side of me. I'm alone. A sound machine hums softly.

The room is empty, no receptionist or other human to speak of. Just then, the door within a door swings open mysteriously, and a short, stocky man with soft eyes, a large nose, and thin lips materializes.

"Mrs. Swift, come on in. I'm Dr. Gordon Ellis."

I sink into a black leather couch, shifting around uncomfortably. Each time it makes a strange sound, and we both smile awkwardly at each other.

"I'm not sure why I'm here. My husband keeps telling me I need medication. I don't know. Maybe he's right, or maybe I just need a job. I have too much time on my hands. Lately, I'm questioning everything, even my own sanity," I say.

"Go on," he says, and he just smiles and tells me it's all right and, in this moment, I feel that it will be all right. Dr. Ellis is like a shot of brandy and he soothes my nerves.

"Freshman year at college, I was attacked walking home from work. It was late. I keep having flashbacks and nightmares. It's been years, and I can't get past it. I don't remember the details and everything is out of sequence in my head. Lately, I feel like I'm in danger all of the time. I keep having panic attacks and I'm out of control. I feel like someone is stalking me. Hunting me and my family. And then, I think I must be going crazy and I'm just stuck in some sort of postpartum panic. I don't know if my memories are even real anymore? Maybe it's just the same blank spaces being filled up by my imagination."

I ask Dr. Ellis, "I mean, why didn't I die that night? I keep asking myself that same question."

"Seraphina, you need help. I can help you," he says.

"Or maybe I'm reaching, trying to preserve the martyr in me. What if deep down, my story is just like everybody else's? At the end of it, I survived an attack. Nothing fresh or new. My thoughts and feelings are dated, like a novel that's gone out of print. And maybe I should just get over it."

Once I start talking, it's impossible stop.

"I wake up every day. I shower. I get dressed. Every day I pretend to be human."

"I pretend I walk in a world that has no flesh or blood. No pain or suffering. In my mind, it's a world of skeletons. Every time I open my eyes, I see what he has done," I say, touching the jagged scar on my head.

"I feel like I'm not making any sense. Am I making sense? Or am I speaking in riddles. I feel like I'm stuck in some sort of trance. I keep seeing blood on my hands. So much blood. I can't tell whose it is anymore."

Soon the words dry up, and I'm screaming. I'm so angry and I can't stop. I just let it all out. I scream so loud, and in my mind, it feels like the world has stopped turning.

I feel like the killer is me. And it always will be. All of that anger, hate and rage flows through me now. Everybody has a dirty little secret. Like a scarlet letter, it burns from the inside. Something they've buried deep until it starts to fester and grow, swollen and filled with pus like an abscessed tooth.

It's not until you cut it open and release all of the bacteria that it actually starts to heal and regenerate.

"That night in Boston, I was raped. I made the choice to abort a child. I never told anyone about the pregnancy. It didn't fit the image of who I wanted to be. The lighter, more beautiful, funny version of Seraphina. And now I'm not sure she isn't gone forever. I can't remember who I used to be."

"Seraphina, it's over. You survived."

"It's like I see his eyes everywhere. He has the eyes of the devil, and all I want to do is run and hide. What do you do if the devil is inside your head?" I say, the tears falling now, the language of my heart breaking.

"The birth of your child, Sky, connected you to that emotional loss. It's hard to love a child born out of rape. You can't keep running. You can't carry the weight of your secret alone. The blood on your hands, the guilt you feel over the loss of that child—you have to forgive yourself to be free of it."

My heart is beating faster, some tribal rhythm, sounds like a beat of a drum.

"So this is what you people do? You're like a preacher or a reverend?" I say, hating him for my vulnerability.

"Are you going to show me how to get to heaven? Because with all of this anger inside, I feel like I'm trapped in hell, and it feels like I'm going insane. Lately, I'm afraid of Harper. And sometimes, I'm so angry at him that I feel like I could kill him. I feel like I'm frozen in this moment, not living in the past or the future, just stuck in this moment. What the hell is wrong with me?"

His voice is soothing. It's as if his hand is reaching inside my body and pulling me out of the wreckage, a disconnected mess of tissue and bones that has come undone. Down and out, I need to be mended.

He explains to me that the voice I hear is the voice of trauma. Dr. Ellis says it's a language he can speak. He can help me translate it, find a way out of it, a way to move forward.

"I don't remember anything from that night. What if I murdered him, slashed him with a broken bottle until he was battered and bloody? Could I possess that kind of anger?"

At that point, I fade in and out of our conversation. My mind moves between flashbacks and feelings of sadness and grief. Dr. Ellis compares my mind to a soldier just home from battle, the chemicals still raging even after the war has ended. That's the voice that has me down, feeling like I'm descending into madness. The official diagnosis is Posttraumatic Stress Disorder. Some people develop it after experiencing a life-threatening event.

I feel naked, stripped down to the side effects of surviving.

"All of those fancy schools, they don't teach a girl how to survive an attack. Or how to live with the memories or about the violence of some men," I say.

"It's over. You have to believe me," he says.

And now I'm sobbing. He makes me believe it's possible to be held together by more than just a needle and thread. I can't imagine who I will be without my armor and chemical reactivity that can light a fire. Finally sewn up, this aching hole in my heart, my sanity hanging by a thread.

My actions are like a pistol, and words cut like a knife. Next time, he wants to talk about my insomnia, the pills and the drinking.

I don't want any more secrets. I don't want any more lies. Stripped down, sewn up, and free.

He tells me to focus on things that make me happy.

So far I have a list of one.

"That's a start," he says, laughing. I should try to fill my mind, occupy it, and let in the light and chemicals that come along with happiness.

He hands me a card with a name on it: Jacob Akani, and his phone number.

"He's expecting your call now."

"Like, right now?"

"You have other plans?"

I frown.

"Seraphina, you need to get stronger, mind and body. I can help with your mind."

I laugh nervously. "So what, Jacob works on my body?"

"See you next week, Seraphina. Remember, think happy thoughts."

Happy feels like an overreach, but I know I can manage *hopeful*. My life has taken a new direction. I can see a bridge to a different place, just off in the distance.

I walk through the wrong door into another office. He has so many doors in this office, I can't find my way out. Dr. Ellis leads me to the right one.

In return, I thank him for picking me up and peeling me off his floor.

I'm going to see Jacob Akani. Because I can't think of a million other things I would rather do. Actually, I can't even think of one.

I'm exhausted. My head is laced with cobwebs from another sleepless night. I enter the subway at Columbus Circle.

It doesn't take long for me to figure out I'm being followed.

I hear Dr. Ellis. "It's the language of trauma. It's all in your mind. Be aware of warning signs. Every flashback starts with a warning."

He said, "Changes in mood, that feeling of pressure in your chest, recognize them early and you can stop the panic and anxiety that follows."

I tell myself to breathe. This isn't real.

But each time I move, he moves with me, and I don't think it's in my head.

I walk quickly, my eyes searching for a diversion. The cover of the *Post* catches my eye. Brooke Beck, the student Harper spoke about who was murdered, smiles at me seductively. I scan the cover story; there's still no suspect.

"Hey! Are you going to buy that?" the beady-eyed vendor asks me.

The man who is stalking me has vanished into thin air. I can't see him anymore. I scan the crowd. My mind is playing tricks on me, making me wonder if he was ever really there at all. The adrenaline is pumping, and I still haven't heard from Harper.

"Sorry. I'll take one, thanks," I say, digging for change.

My mind is active and on overdrive. The train pulls up, and I move forward with the crush of commuters. One-track mind, I sit and try to distract myself from the panic attack, my unwanted companion on this ride.

Harper hasn't found Brooke Beck's killer and I know that will gnaw at him. It will chip away at his fragile ego until it becomes his obsession.

The funeral for Brooke Beck wasn't well attended. Most of the pews were empty. She was only nineteen years old. It is impossible to know if she traveled or had seen any more of the world than what was put in front of her.

In my mind, death is a lot like dreaming or the setting of the sun, with a natural beauty and rhythm to it. I guess that's the truth about trauma, and maybe even a silver lining, if only a thin and fragile one, at best. Surviving makes you better, more sensitive to the pain of others, but not happier because some scars stay etched in your soul.

Trauma reminds you of every platitude—that life is precious, that money and power are overrated, and that all we really have together is this moment, the blink of an eye, amid the vastness of time and space.

I can't take my eyes off a close-up picture of a young girl, lingering near the closed casket.

Her rich, dark hair tumbles over her shoulders, the curve of her heart-shaped lips and voluptuous lines of her body, like a vintage Hollywood pinup girl.

She has eyes like sunlight and sapphires, their depth reflecting a melancholy mood.

These aren't the types of girls who play it safe. They take risks. They own every moment. I'm shocked to read the article, excerpts from Brooke's diary about her life as a highly paid escort, and how she used it to pay for grad school. Brooke had put up a profile even before her plane touched down in New York City, lured into a world where sex and money mingle.

My intuition is picking up on something else, a presence beyond the whore who was murdered and the cops trying to put the pieces together.

Harper is lying. Did he have an affair with Brooke Beck? She wasn't just a student in need of help. My intuition is picking up on something beyond the cracks in the road and the lies that Brooke Beck told to pay her way through Yale. I can feel something disturbing. I can't back it up with any logic or reason.

It's just a feeling.

Eight

SERAPHINA AND JACOB

I knock on the door. It swings open, and the receptionist invites me into the studio. Out the window is a view of the sweeping New York skyline. On the wall is a sign that reads, "You've Got Three Choices in Life. Give up, give in, or give it all you've got."

My gaze slides past her to the silver punching bags hanging from the wall, the black padded gloves, and the free weights that line the floor of the padded walls.

"Seraphina? I thought I recognized your voice. We met at the gun shop."

"How did you know I would be coming?"

"I didn't know it was you. Gordon just said he was sending someone over for training."

"So you work at the gun shop?"

"No, I was just helping out my cousin. They just had a baby, and he's not sleeping much. I haven't been back since that day. It's good to see you. You probably have no idea why you're here, right?"

"No. None."

"I know. Gordon likes to do that. He thinks he's Yoda, the Jedi master."

Even in workout gear, I can see the outline of Jacob's chiseled abs and biceps, the kind of fitness that takes dedication and hard work to perfect. His salt-and-pepper hair is cut military style. Jacob is strong and gallant, with an irresistible laugh.

"Seraphina, some types of trauma change the brain chemistry." He gives me a Richard Gere-style wink, smoky and confident; it's as if the endorphins flow through him into me. I'm feeling energized and in good spirits.

"So you'll help me change the chemistry in my brain back to normal?"

"No, I can't do that, but I can teach you how to use it, to feel safer, and I can teach you how to fight to win. Go put these on," he says, throwing me a black T-shirt and shorts.

"I'm good. I can just wear this." After several weeks of self-induced semi-isolation, I find this experience more than a little daunting. It reminds me uncomfortably of the way I felt on the first day of high school.

He eyeballs my black dress and leggings.

"You're a control freak, aren't you? I'm moving too fast for you? Sit down." He puts an arm around my shoulder and leads me to a wooden bench.

Jacob is overwhelmingly charming. Even in my exhausted, emotionally whiplashed state of being, I can feel my cheeks heating up as I begin to blush.

"I teach Krav Maga, a form of self-defense and physical training developed by the Israeli army. It's based on the body's natural instincts. It's actually about problem solving and a no-nonsense system designed to bring out the fight in you. This is the opposite of what the world teaches you. You need to be fierce and aggressive."

"But I'm not that strong, and I'm small."

"You will get stronger, and in this case, size doesn't matter."

We both laugh, which cuts the tension.

"It's based on instinct and using what you've got to win, above all else, to stay safe and win."

"I don't understand."

"I mean, you have to attack vulnerable areas like eyes, jaw, throat, liver—anywhere you can strike for maximum damage with minimal effort and strength. You're stronger than you know, Seraphina. Think about it. You are a survivor."

This brings tears to my eyes. He notices, and in his eyes, I see empathy, not pity. Jacob is a force, and I feel as if I have been brought to him for a reason.

"Its origins can be traced back to World War II and a young Jewish athlete, Imi Lichtenfeld, who organized a group of young men to patrol his community and defend against attackers. Israeli military leaders quickly noticed his fighting skills and put him in charge of training the military elite's fighting forces."

My mind wanders. I think if I exhaust myself, I will sleep tonight, finally overwhelming my mind's agitation with my body's exhaustion. I make myself a promise. Just for one night.

"It combines the most effective techniques of boxing, aikido, judo, wrestling, and jujitsu into one military discipline that emphasizes fluid motion and simultaneous defense and attacks to an assailant's soft tissue and pressure points."

I vow to stop drinking. I won't take any more pills. After all, I've got nothing to lose.

"Let's get started. If you're not interested, you can take off. I'm here to help you."

I know what I want from Jacob. I'm not exactly sure he's willing to put that on the table.

"How do you know if you don't try? Maybe you already have killer instincts," Jacob says.

In the bathroom, I slip into the black shorts and shirt. My phone shows that I missed a call from Harper. An emptiness fills up my chest. My head feels like it's going to explode.

He must know he is playing with fire, coming home late with the stink of another woman. If Harper is cheating on me, I will find out and show him no mercy.

I wonder when he started fucking her—that nasty, vampy, desperate, slutty poacher. I bet she likes tequila shots and takes every inch of him. The type with "daddy issues" always do. I bet she lets him do anything: doggy style, hair pulling, ball gags, and all of it. I'm sure she is a freak, because that type always is, and I plan on breaking her. I will stalk my husband in pursuit of the truth. And when I find him, last night's bite will feel like a warm hug.

"So you can teach me to be a bad-ass human weapon," I say.

"Pretty much."

"And you know my history, clearly. But I don't know yours."

"I'm also a firearms enthusiast."

"Perfect," I say.

"We start with shadowboxing to warm up the core. Left-leg-forward fighting stance. Good. Hands up, chin height. Now, just block me. Always keep moving in fighting stance."

I freeze.

"You have to keep moving forward, Seraphina. I know it's hard when someone is coming at you. Think about it: what if it was up to you to protect your daughter? You always fight to win. See if you can hit me."

Then I think of Harper and his slut. I feel as if I have to fight. Each time my hand strikes out and I make contact, it brings me peace, more than anything I've ever found at the bottom of a bottle. I let it flow. My nails digging into my palms, pure hatred flowing, head up and strong, the anger comes in intense flashes.

Then I get carried away by the emotion, and my hands drop. He moves in and picks me up, fast and furious, and drops me on the mat.

"You just lost."

"You're stronger," I say.

"That's an excuse."

I laugh.

"That's my rule. Change the way you think."

"Okay, sorry."

"And don't apologize either. It's the same thing as an excuse."

"I get the idea. I'm tired. I've got to get home," I say, getting up to leave.

Jacob puts his hand on my shoulder and says, "I'm glad you came, Seraphina."

Now, in his words, I think I hear pity.

"That was good. First lesson and all. I've seen worse. And I know it's a lot to take in. You have to commit to it."

I change back into my street clothes.

"Call me if you want to come back, kid."

There is no Zen in Krav Maga. You train to have a mind that is sharp and accurate, a body that is toned and taut because you have pushed it to its physical limits. It's a skill that takes time, dedication, and practice.

"Bye, Jacob," I say, looking into his deep, smiling eyes.

He puts his arms around me. I take a deep breath in; his musky, spicy scent overtakes me.

"Bye, kid," he says, his voice tense and husky, and we both linger just a little too long.

I feel as if I have been staring down a long, dark tunnel, and finally, I can see a glimmer of light.

Over time, I will learn how to move and think with precision. I will set these things to muscle memory.

As I walk out the door, I see a photograph on the wall, a fist covered in blood.

The sign below reads, "I will walk in peace."

Nine
HARPER AND JESSA

"Closer. We're getting closer," says Belle. Baffled for a moment, Harper orders his usual scrambled eggs and toast.

The sun is almost up, a blanket of light, the air crisp and chilly.

"Where did you sleep last night, and what happened to your neck?"

"The guesthouse, which didn't suck. And Seraphina happened to my neck."

He laughs.

"What did you get from Jessa? Anything?"

Too much, his subconscious laughs at him.

"Nothing more than we already had," Harper says, lying to Belle for the first time ever.

"Brooke Beck used the ID Aries77. I followed her threads all night, and I've got something. She was really going at it with ZodiacNW the night before the murder. Threats and insults. It got pretty heated," Harper tells Belle.

Harper had printed everything and saved it on a hard drive.

"ZodiacNW has a strong following and high engagement with users. He cracked a big case, a disappearance of a seven-year-old girl from Zoar, Ohio, named Maria Oscarn," says Belle.

"Go on," Harper says.

"They found her body five months later, or what was left of it, in a field. There was no DNA, no confession by the killer. He solved it based on an anonymous tip. Zodiac looked into routes driven by truckers who traveled through Ohio and Pennsylvania. A fifteen-year-old girl, a hitchhiker, came forward online and described how she had been robbed at knifepoint and escaped the man he identified as Ron Reimy. He was facing ten counts of aggravated murder, six of kidnapping, four of rape, and two of aggravated robbery when he was found dead on the side of Route 20 from a gunshot wound to the head."

"Did you get a subpoena for the IP addresses?"

"Of course. We requested the IP address and identification of the computer."

"Fine. I'll drive," Harper says. "I can drive."

Harper gives Belle a death glance. Still fighting, but unlike Seraphina, in the case of Belle, Harper always wins. Harper pays the check, and they get into a black SUV and drive over the Brooklyn Bridge, toward Dead Horse Bay. Back in the 1850s, this was the area of the waterfront that served as the final destination for the city's carriage horses. Horse carcasses were delivered by barge to gigantic bone-boiling plants and processed into glue and fertilizer. The factories closed down after a series of natural disasters.

Over the last sixty years, the man-made beach at Dead Horse Bay has slowly eroded. You can still find the shoreline littered with bottles and artifacts.

"Five more minutes," Harper says, according to the GPS.

SEEING RED

They turn into Jacob Riis Park, an old abandoned lot, the building aged and rusted, split-level and made of steel.

The beach is quiet and eerie in the dead of winter and the feeling almost postapocalyptic.

"What the hell?" Belle says, looking out over the dashboard.

Deep breath, hands on their guns, they enter the abandoned building. It's empty, aside from an open laptop in the center of the room. The light streams in through the blown-out windows, making it feel even more surreal. Harper turns the power on and keeps his eyes glued to the screen. He clicks on the only file on the desktop.

When he hits enter, a cipher comes up on the screen. It looks like a classic Caesar Cipher. Easy to decrypt, each letter of the message is replaced by the letter three positions later in the alphabet.

Harper's cell starts to ring. It's Jessa calling. He will have to deal with her later. He silences it and takes out a paper and pen.

"Just call out the letters to me."

"K."

"K translates to H."

Back and forth they go until Harper has it all down. The first clue:

Heaven has no rage like love turned to hatred, Nor hell hath no fury like a woman scorned.

Belle shakes his head. "A paraphrased poem? Is this some sort of joke?"

"I have no idea what this cryptic shit is all about."

"You think it's a hoax?" Belle remarks.

"I don't. I think it's a move, like chess. And we're up."

For Harper, there is always a flaw, even in the best-laid human plans. He just has to be patient and wait for it. He needs to stay positive and focused.

Belle's phone rings. He picks it up and puts it on speaker.

"Where are you?" Lara's tone is sharp.

"We are at the warehouse."

"We've got a positive ID from the vigil in front of Brooke Beck's apartment."

"Thanks, Lara. We're on our way back," says Belle. "Harp, over here."

He makes his way over to Belle, who is holding a large gel capsule with a brownish powder in it.

"What is this?" Belle asks.

"I don't know. Let's get it to the lab."

Harper looks over at Belle, and suddenly his smile is gone.

"What's wrong?"

"I'm not seeing the connection in all of this? You?"

"Nope."

As they drive back over the Brooklyn Bridge, its suspension wires and cables remind him of a marionette. He hates getting played like a puppet. He feels out of control, like someone is pulling his strings.

Back at the police station, FBI Agent Walthrop stands in front of a whiteboard filled with details and bloody crime scene photos. The room reeks of coffee and sweat under the flickering glow of the fluorescent white lighting. Lara Kane has her head down on the white table, clearly trying to collect her thoughts and link together the confusing pieces of the puzzle.

"Can you get a rush on this?" Belle says, handing Lara the brown gel capsule to investigate.

Lara has the video pulled up on her computer from the night of Brooke's vigil, frozen at the image of a red- headed male in his early twenties, leaving flowers on the steps of the brownstone.

Lara says, "Meet Johnny Finn, a registered sex offender. He's a local contractor hired to do a renovation on the neighboring brownstone."

Lara continues, "Finn says he was just Brooke's friend. Johnny was at a bar less than ten miles away on the night of the murder."

"Nice job. Is he here?" Belle says.

"We seized the laptop, and we put a digital tracker on it. He's waiting for questioning," Lara says.

As part of the FBI's Next Generation Identification System, the database houses millions of photographs they can use to identify a face in a crowd and track them through the facial-recognition computer program.

"Johnny, we just need to ask you where you were on the night of Brooke Beck's murder," Harper says.

"I was at the Union House. Grabbing a beer."

"When was the last time you saw Brooke Beck?"

"I went to her apartment the day she was murdered, but she wasn't there. She was at school."

Harper glares at Johnny and asks, "How did you get in?"

"She left a key in the umbrella stand near the front door. She wasn't home much, so I used the place to clean up before I went out. I work in construction."

"That's awfully nice of her. Was she your girlfriend?" Harper asks.

"No."

"Did she know you are a registered sex offender?"

"That was something that happened a long time ago, and it was never my intention to hurt anyone. I didn't murder Brooke Beck. She was my friend. That's all."

Harper doesn't get the feeling this kid is capable of murder. Johnny Finn lacked the intelligence and sophistication to pull off something like this.

Harper continues, "Why don't you tell us how you ended up on the Megan's Law registry and convicted of sex crimes against children."

"It was a hard time in my life. I was lost. I didn't know what to do with myself. I felt like I had no future. So a bunch of my friends and I decided to take LSD in Central Park. We wanted a spiritual experience."

Johnny stops and sucks his teeth in for a moment, as if he isn't sure he wants to go any further.

He goes on, "I started hallucinating and thought I was going swimming. I took off all of my clothes and climbed into the fountain near the Boat House. A preschool class was on a field trip, and I was arrested for indecent exposure."

Harper isn't sure this is the truth, but anything this stupid just has to be true.

Johnny says, "People like you have ruined my life. I can't go anywhere without that one mistake following me. I can't hold down a job, much less get a job that's worth anything. It's all on my record, and it was just an accident."

"I'm sorry. That's a tough break. And before that you spent some time in the army?"

"Yes. I was discharged after a suicide attempt. I have PTSD. I'm sure you know that already."

Harper trusts his gut feeling that Brooke's murderer is still out there.

"Yes. I think we're done here. Thanks for coming in. We'll be in touch if we need to ask you anything else. You can pick up your computer on the way out," Belle says.

"Harp, this pill is Ibogaine; it's a psychoactive alkaloid from the root bark of the central West African shrub, iboga."

"What's it used for?" Belle says.

"Well, it's illegal in this country, but it's used in other countries to treat heroin or any other long-term opiate addiction. The side effects are brutal: nausea, vomiting, and violent, mind-warping hallucinations. Either you detox or the hallucinogenic trip will kill you. It's legal in some countries, controversial but effective."

"How did they get their hands on it here?"

"You can still get it on the dark web. They may have busted Silk Road, the drug bazaar of choice, but there are a dozen more vendors just like that where you can still go."

"Anything else?" Belle asks.

"It does have another use, as a shamanistic ritual. It's a traditional African spiritual practice that induces what they call an awakened dream state. It provides insight into past traumatic events that can lead to addiction and negative thinking. It's sort of a psychological reboot."

"You mean I can fast-forward years of psychotherapy with this one little pill?"

"It's a very powerful drug and hard to regulate, based on a traditional African spiritual practice that focuses on ancestor worship and a direct connection to God."

"Do you think we're dealing with some sort of ritual crime or secret society?" Lara asks.

"No, I think we're dealing with a psychopath who works alone, and one that seems to know a lot about botanical poisons and psychedelics."

Harper has heard enough. He doesn't know what to make of the psychedelics and wonders if they are being used as some sort of herbal date-rape drug. There is no way that tool, Johnny Finn, could commit murder.

Harper is having trouble focusing on anything other than Jessa. His mind is racing, obsessing over her lies. His anger, like lightning, strikes hard and fast.

By the time Jessa texts Harper, he's already parked across the street from her apartment in SoHo, smoking a cigarette out the window of his car, just watching her.

He tries to calm himself as he walks across Greene Street. He tends to lose control when he is this angry. He can feel his teeth grinding, his whole body tense, and his eyes bulging with rage. As he gets into the elevator, he is reminded of their affair.

He starts to breathe slowly, in and out, and by the time the doors open into Jessa's apartment, he is more at peace.

Jessa is waiting for him, arms folded, hair tightly bound in a sexy braid, and her white silk shirt is just a hint transparent.

"Hi, Harp."

"So what is your real name? Jessa or Jessica?" Harper says. "Maybe you can start by telling me who I was with last night?" he asks, using a carefully controlled tone.

"My real name is Jessa. My escort name is Jessica, but I'm guessing you figured that out."

"What does 'real' even mean to a girl like you?" he says with derision.

"Is that what you wanted last night, to see the 'real' me? Because men like you are so narcissistic they see whatever it is they want to see."

She is trying to provoke him. This girl has no fear. Now he's angry again, eyes like steel, lips curling into a snarl.

"Do you accept money in exchange for sex, Jessa?"

"You know I can't answer that."

"Can't or won't?" His eyes are cold and flinty. "How about I give you a free pass just like you gave me one when you fucked me in the elevator last night."

"Fuck you, Harper."

He grabs her face roughly in one hand and brings it close to his. "Don't test me, Jessa. You will lose. I promise."

Her breath hitches. She pushes back, her nails digging into his skin.

The heat between them is growing. He hates himself, but he still wants her, despite her bad choices. He watches her, now vulnerable, walls down. She is biting at the bottom of her lip, holding back tears.

"You're scaring me, Harper."

He can feel the blood course through his veins, mind lost and twisting. The lack of sleep is wearing him down, still haunted by last night's vivid dream.

The open moon shining its silvery light over quicksand, the surface of it shimmers and shakes. A hand rises up from the center; he reaches in, fingers slipping away like grains of sand.

In his dream, as he moves in closer, a head rises from the quicksand. He sees himself drowning in silent terror.

He catches himself and lets go of Jessa, breathing, trying to relax. Without words, he moves slowly toward the living room, taking a seat on the couch.

"I'm sorry," she says honestly. "I felt a real connection to you, and I didn't want to ruin it with the truth." She sits down next to him.

He lets out a bittersweet laugh.

He looks at her curled up on the couch, like an exotic animal, well worth his capture.

"You're so beautiful," Harper says. "I just don't understand why you do it?" His gaze is distracted by the glow from the streetlights outside. It should be so easy for him to walk away.

"I like the adrenaline rush of it, I guess. I like sex."

His eyes search hers, wanting so much to understand, to possess her, but knowing he never will.

"Aren't you worried you're going to end up dead?" he asks.

Even with her darkest secrets exposed, she is confident, fierce, and dangerous.

"I don't know, Harp. Aren't you worried that you're going to end up dead? Are we really so different?" Jessa says this with a radiant, crooked smile, her eyes blazing through him. The heat between them is charged and electric.

"Maybe I'm an accident of nature, but I prefer the rush of the unknown," she says, her breathing rhythmic and shallow. She leans in, her body lightly touching him, and whispers softly, "In another time, I could be your royal mistress and you my king, and there would be no scandal. It would be my job to pleasure you."

She provokes him with her mouth, her eyes, her breasts. The strength of his desire is no longer under his control.

He touches her face gently and strokes her cheek. She pushes him away, not wanting his tenderness, wanting him for his strength and to dominate her.

He can tell she wants to be punished, so he points to the bedroom. "Crawl to it."

She smiles and gets down on her hands and knees, enjoying the game.

He watches her body move, graceful and voluptuous. He bends her back over the bed, unbuttoning her shirt, removing her lace lingerie. He runs his hands over her breasts, thighs, and torso, covering her body with his. She trembles at the strength of his touch. He rips off her skirt as if it is made of paper.

He bites at her nipples, twisting her as if she is made of elastic, until she begs for him.

"Not yet," he says, ruling over her like a king, and she takes great pleasure, as if it is her responsibility to honor and revere him.

"Look at me," he says, every kiss adding to the warmth of their bodies, until slowly he eases into her, the rhythm of her pleasure mounting until her need to be taken and satisfied is her only unconscious desire.

He watches her, worships her as she rolls onto him, undulating, bodies fused together, both ravenously hungry for each other.

They climax together, a blaze of ecstasy ripping through his body.

She takes his hand and puts it to her cheek. He runs his fingers through her hair and brings her close with light kisses all over her body.

He is still aroused; the excitement pulses through him, but this time he pulls away.

"Stay. Just for the night," she says.

She rolls over next to him, twisting every inch of her body around him, as if he needs more than her body to convince him.

"If we lived in a different time, your marriage would only be a matter of politics and preserving bloodlines," she says.

"What do you really think can happen here, Jessa?"

"Whatever you're comfortable with. I'm open to anything," she says, clearly talking about her body.

"Listen, I wanted to get away from my parents. I just didn't want to have to depend on anyone for money. I only do it once or twice a month. I enjoy it. For just one night, I get to be whoever I want to be. It's not my—forever plan. It's just for right now."

"Well, you better rethink your major, because I don't see medieval studies as the off-ramp you're looking for," he says, with laughter dancing in his eyes.

"Look, I'm not sure I can protect you, Jessa. I need to know who else is involved. Did someone put you up to this? I can keep your name out of things, if you can give me more information about Brooke and the night of the murder. We think she may have had information as to who the Renaissance Killer might be."

"Renaissance Killer?"

"Yes, a serial killer responsible for murdering women in the sex trade in Boston. The case went cold, but the poison used in Brooke's murder makes us think the cases are connected."

"Don't you think I would tell you if I had any more information?" she asks innocently.

"I think you've got a mind of your own. I think you do what you want, and you've convinced yourself you're in control and you can handle the pain, maybe even enjoy it. Any pain other than the one that comes from living an ordinary life," he says.

He can see her mind working, trying to come to terms with some choice she has to make.

Harper isn't proud of this trait. His greatest professional strength makes him a flawed and deplorable human being. He always knows how to push people, just hard enough to make them break.

"You're playing a dangerous game, Jessa. Trust me, I've seen how it ends. The story will break, and you will be exposed for prostitution. If not tomorrow, then the day after that, and I can't protect you."

They dress in silence.

To Harper, truth is the only thing that matters because it almost always leads to justice; more than his feelings for Jessa or the guilt and anger he feels toward himself for losing Seraphina a little at a time.

Justice matters above all else, or at least that's what he tells himself.

It makes it easier for him to contain his emotions as he walks out the door. Jessa walks him to his car. She surprises him with a kiss. He pushes her away gently and instead holds her tightly, as if he may never let her go. He feels alive with Jessa.

Harper's eyes fill with tenderness. He is intoxicated by her and can't handle the thought of leaving her. The passion takes over, and he kisses her in the middle of the street before getting in his car and driving away.

If only Harper had looked back.

Ten

SERAPHINA AND JESSA

I'm standing on a corner in SoHo, watching Harper kiss his whore, really leaning into it, giving her every inch of him. She has that sexy, tousled, already-came-hither look about her—the one that I used to have when Harper and I first started sleeping together. The worst part is, he looks happy, young, and carefree. She flips her head back, and I can almost hear her girlish giggle, a sprinkle of laughter like a bullet through my heart.

She doesn't look like a home-wrecker or porn star. She just looks like a girl, the kind you would see walking into any trendy gallery or upscale restaurant in SoHo, having a drink at the bar. She is very much a girl like me—or at least, the girl I used to be.

I start to shake and shiver from the feeling of rage as it courses through my suburban veins. The light from the streetlamp exposes all of their sins. His whore sighs, releasing a small, steamy cloud into the night air. If she thinks she's tired now, just wait until she spends her days trying to live up to me. Any attempts to send him back will be marked "return to sender."

No, she isn't at all how I pictured her to be, all cheap and desperate. Not standing here, a work of art, with her slinky black skirt, tight body, and heels as tall as the Empire State. She looks sleek and sophisticated, a disguise to conceal her true identity as a home-wrecking, husband-thieving whore.

So much for my parents' theory that cheaters never prosper, because it looks like Harper is feeling rich as a king, while I stand here freezing, poor as a pauper.

I'm humiliated, and my stomach churns. Now I'm wasting more than time; I'm wasting precious tears. They fall from my eyes like icicles hanging from the windows above. I can imagine one breaking free, plunging into him, the weight of it so heavy and damaging, proving even new love isn't indestructible.

It is a cold night; snowflakes whip and whirl as if dancing in the wind.

All smoky eyes and heaving bosom, she's the kind of girl who shops at Kiki de Montparnasse for lingerie, a girl who could have been Man Ray's muse. She is so sexual and provocative, it's as if she's dripping with honey.

This girl has gotten sloppy seconds, and my husband, well, he's just gotten sloppy. After leaving Jacob earlier, I called Harper's office, and his new assistant gave me this address.

She said, "It's really no problem. He's just working, and I'm sure he would love to see you."

My life is being clever, showing me what could have been if I had only opened a different door. Any door would have been better than the one I walked through and my life with Harper. All of these thoughts run through my mind as my body propels forward, as if tied to an engine. Until I'm standing in the doorway of her building, staring at her buzzer.

I ring.

"How did I know you would be back? I'll send the elevator down," she says seductively.

It arrives. I get in, heart pounding, an unnatural stillness to my body.

The door opens into her apartment. There is no turning back now, the horror of seeing my own confusion and grasping at the straws of it.

"Who are you?"

"Not my husband, and I'm guessing that's who you were expecting. I'm Seraphina."

"Jessa. I'm Jessa. He's not here anymore. He may even be home by now," she says nervously, looking at the open elevator door and hoping I will turn and go.

Instead, I step inside.

The empty living room is sexy and modern. I can see Harper here, settling in and happy. My eyes scan the art, books that line the shelves, Milton, Shakespeare, and Marlowe. Jessa has pinned her hair back. There is something very familiar about her. My mind whirls like the blades of a helicopter, and then I realize why she looks so familiar.

She is the friend of that NYU student, Brooke Beck, the one who was murdered in her apartment. I remember seeing Jessa's picture in the pages of the *Post*.

Those sapphire eyes, so wide open and haunted, her face is etched in pain. She has a dangerous beauty and one that is hard to forget.

As I look around, everything in this apartment holds the promise of sex. The air still smells thick with it. I move toward the window. I can feel my thoughts layering, one on top of the other.

"Listen, I don't know how you're going to take this, and it really doesn't matter to me. I want to let you know that the man you are fucking is mine. Everything from the clothes on his back to the bed he sleeps in, all of it is mine. I can see you're young and beautiful. You own a lot of expensive things. You must even love some of them."

I move toward a lamp. It has a cobalt-blue base made from blown glass. I pick it up and hold it, balancing it with one hand.

"Some things are delicate. Maybe you've taken them for granted, but deep down you still love them, and then some stranger comes along and breaks it."

I let the light drop to the floor. It shatters everywhere, each piece cloudy, like sea glass. The light goes out, leaving us standing with only the glow from the streetlamp.

"I think you should leave before I call the police," she says.

"Now I know you're a whore, but are you also a prostitute? Just like your friend … Brooke, right? I can't really see Harper going for that sort of thing."

I watch the storm settle behind her eyes, the darkness that moves through her in seconds, her fear fading to anger.

She moves closer to me, like a cat on the prowl, and sits down next to me.

"Don't judge me, Seraphina. Maybe I'm just like you, minus the rich daddy who paid your way to mediocrity. We really aren't so different. If you would allow yourself a little more fun, just a little more freedom, maybe your husband wouldn't be fucking someone else."

She puts her hand on my leg. There's something about Jessa, so alive and passionate.

"I'm nothing like you, Jessa," I say.

"Women like you wouldn't exist without women like me. Most of the men I see are married. They just need somebody to listen, maybe burn off a little stress. I help them with that. It's all business to me, and sex is only a small piece of it. So your judgment, Seraphina, it has no place in my conscience."

SEEING RED

I can feel my head scream, like the thrash of the wind against the windowpane. I turn to go.

"Maybe we can help each other," she whispers, moving in closer and brushing her lips against mine. "I can show you what I do for Harper. I can teach you."

Blood-red anger rises up, a tidal wave of destruction, and I lose control, pushing Jessa backward with all of my strength.

She falls and hits her head on the metal edge of the coffee table. Her breathing is shallow and faint.

This girl even makes broken beautiful. Her eyes are closed, peaceful and angelic.

I have crossed the line of logic and reason, and now I'm running like hell, with no hope of going back. My heart is lodged firmly in my throat. I'm so tired, and yet I keep running.

I hit the down elevator button. I look around to make sure nobody sees me leave. My heart is beating, and my anxiety is rising.

A stellar collision is the coming together of two stars, their competing gravitational forces throwing off gas and matter as they collide. Each burns bright, pulsating heat and light. Some will form a union, one that doubles in size and strength.

But for some, the forces of their interior are too strong, each star exploding, and what remains is a black hole.

I dig my cell phone out of my bag and dial Harper's number.

"We need to talk. Where are you?" I say to Harper, my voice windy, almost musical.

"I'm driving. I'm almost home."

"Stay home. I'm on my way," I say.

He is a liar and a cheat. I hail a taxi.

"Can you take me to 87 West River Road in Rumson?"

"Where?" He rolls his eyes.

"It's off the Garden State Parkway."

"Fine. Get in." He plugs the address into Waze.

I can feel myself falling down a black hole, a place where some say time even stands still. I'm not falling in love; I'm falling in anger and hate. Every time I think I've hit rock bottom, I fall even farther down.

I call Birdie to check on Sky and tell her I'm on my way home. I slip my phone back into the pocket of my jacket, and I find the card Carter had given me earlier at Penn Station with his phone number on it. If I was going to cheat on my husband, I wouldn't waste it on someone random. I want revenge. It would have to be someone who would drive the knife in deeper and twist it. Someone like Carter, who went against his grain; that would burn a hole in his heart.

The call goes straight to voicemail.

Some love dies a natural death. Some love has the life choked out of it, denied its most basic needs, like oxygen.

I leave a message for Carter. "Hi, it's Seraphina, and it was great to run into you on the train this morning. I would love to get together. Give me a call."

I smile and close my eyes.

In my mind, I can see Jessa, gasping for air, fighting for her last breath. My hands are around her neck, eyes bulging and veins throbbing as she drops to the floor. My mind plays tricks on me. I can see the terror in her eyes as she thrashes and claws, begging for me to let her live. Even as she takes her last breath, she is still fighting me.

If truth is only an illusion, I'm no longer sure what is real. I remember, when the elevator door opened, I turned back when I should have run, and the rest of it is now damage that can no longer be undone.

"Miss."

Someone is shaking me.

"Miss, this is 87 West River Road. We're here."

Eleven
SERAPHINA AND HARPER

The light in the bedroom is on, and I can see Harper pacing. He catches a glimmer of light from the headlights. He moves toward the window and takes a drink. The house is soundless. The night is unseasonably warm, and a fog hangs heavy in the sky. It feels like I can fade away into the darkness of it.

The distressed wood and stone, chestnut bricks hand cut and stacked make our home feel like it belongs in another place and time. My mind goes blank, and my heart stumbles to catch up with the moment, as I climb the stairs toward the end of my marriage.

I stand in the doorway, arms folded, watching Harper pack his clothes. He has a lit cigarette dangling from his mouth. He turns toward me; our eyes lock, fierce and ready for battle.

"So that's it. You're just going?" I say.

Harper doesn't like messes, so he's careful with his words, even withholding. The betrayal and damage are the roots that grow from our love and affection.

"I don't want you to go. At least not right now. We need to talk," I say.

His lips tighten, and his words trickle out of his mouth slowly. He picks up a stack of white dress shirts, clean and pressed, carefully packing them away in his suitcase, not lifting his eyes to look at me.

"Stop speaking in code, Seraphina. Say what you have to say. You always make everything so complicated."

I smile, and it's bright and cold, laced with poison. "Okay. Then why don't you start by telling me about the other woman you're fucking, Harper. I think you owe me that. Or am I just making things complicated again?"

He looks at me, his lips tightening, his body coiled like a rattlesnake, tense and just waiting for the right moment to strike.

"You kissed her, Harp. Right there in the middle of the street. Have you lost your mind? You've always been selfish, but you've never been stupid and crazy."

Harper stops packing and takes the cigarette from between his lips, crushing it in the ashtray until the embers fade.

Harper could never understand why I wouldn't let him smoke in his own fucking house. He smokes around the baby, not all the time but every once in a while, with no regard for her health or mine. He has to do it all his way. He's so controlling and selfish, and now a cheater.

"I'm crazy? Are you kidding me? You need serious help. You aren't a healthy person. You aren't fit to be a mother. You need medication. The nightmares and paranoia, it's like you're in a constant manic state, buying things on the Internet. If you're not sick, well then you're just a spoiled, unhappy bitch, and I'm done with you and your negativity."

"You're a liar and a cheat. You're acting like the spoiled child. You slept with someone else! Don't even try to blame all of this on me." I can hear my voice raised and angry.

He zips up his suitcase. He won't look at me. He turns to go. I stand in front of it, blocking his way. I'm not prepared to let him go on his own terms. I need to find out all of his lies, the filthy secrets he has been hiding, like Brooke Beck and Jessa Dante.

"How many others?" I ask, snatching his cell phone from his hands and scrolling through his texts.

"Give it back. Now."

He tries to take it back, but I throw it against the wall, shattering the glass of his iPhone screen.

"Are you in love with her? Come on, Harper. I deserve some answers. How long have you been cheating on me with that bitch?"

He manages to get his hand around the doorknob. "Fuck you, Harper. You're a coward, just like your father. A cheater and a drunk with one foot out the door."

He stops to let the words seep in and burn, and then he turns, throwing his suitcase at the wall. It opens, clothes spilling out everywhere.

He faces me, eyes blazing. He charges toward me and grabs my arms roughly. I'm filled with adrenaline, rage, and a merciless need for revenge. Arms pinned, I have no armor, so all I can think to do is spit in his face. He lets go, and I grab his drink and throw it at him. The glass smashes into a million jagged pieces.

He backs away in disgust as if I'm vile.

"Why are you doing this? I'm giving you back your freedom. At the hospital, you said it's who we are together that's your problem," Harper says.

"Well, then I have to let you go, Seraphina. Because I can't stand who you've become. The more I try to love you, the more I feel myself suffocating."

"I accept your apology."

"And lately, I don't love you. I can't even pretend to tolerate you. You're completely insane."

"You don't care about me. You're not willing to do what it takes to make our marriage work. You're nothing but a lying, cheating psychopath, a loser."

"Shut up, you crazy bitch!" he says as he raises his fist. He catches himself before he takes a swing and pushes me out of the way. I fall onto the broken glass, and I look down at my hands, now bloody and raw, just like in my dream. I'm scratching, hitting, and clawing. He's covered in the blood from my hands. I want him to feel my pain.

Then I hear the sound of my daughter crying, her voice a fallen melody, a battle cry I recognize from my own childhood.

"I'm sorry. I didn't mean for any of this to happen," Harper says.

"Just get out. I don't want you here anymore." A million jagged pieces of glass rip through my heart, my pain reflected in the sound of him leaving.

I hear Birdie singing a soft lullaby, the notes filling in the spaces between my sadness.

I am bloody, broken, and bruised.

So I stop fighting, and in that moment of silence, I surrender. The emotions gush out of me, a rush of tears and wrath, a ramble of words and feelings, things I have never dared to think or say.

I love my parents, even though their pain and fear haunted my childhood and left me with scars, the kind that take up too much room in my heart. Scars that leave a mark on anyone who tries to love me.

Harper does not know that I have drawn a target on his back. I am not like my mother, hiding behind vanity and superficiality, suffering and screaming behind closed doors. I will bring our fight into the light. I pull the glass from my hands and clean my wounds, wrapping them, as if I'm a boxer ready for the next round. It is Harper who taught me the rules of the game.

He said, "The greatest knockouts are the ones that touch you, tear at you, heart and soul. They take a combination of physical power and mental brilliance, precision, planning, and balance. The more connected you are to the fight, the more pain you feel as your opponent goes down."

There's nothing more dangerous than a woman scorned who takes pleasure in pain.

Twelve
HARPER

Harper wakes up at 5:00 a.m., head pounding. He'd fallen asleep in the car; he checks for his phone, only to remember it shattered along with his marriage the night before. He had passed out in the car last night. He had flirted with alcoholism all week, but last night he officially committed.

Seraphina was angry, and last night hit them both like a wrecking ball. He could easily rationalize Jessa. She was only a side effect of his problems with Seraphina. Jessa struck like lightning at his heart.

He grabs coffee and a bagel and heads north on the Garden State, arriving at the office early, expecting to find peace and quiet, not a room full of strangers.

"I've been calling you, Harp. Where have you been?" Belle asks, looking frantic and anxious.

"Sorry. I was dealing with a family emergency. I need a new phone, and while you're at it, a new assistant."

"You remember FBI Agent Walthrop," Belle said.

"Please tell me you have news on Brooke Beck's case," Harper says.

Belle has his computer open to an e-mail; he slides it over to Harper. "Can you click on the hyperlink?"

He clicks on the mouse, and an image comes up on the computer screen.

It's small, and the picture is grainy; it's some sort of street cam. He can see pedestrians weaving in and out. The camera moves in closer. It's a video from last night, with Jessa, locked in a heated embrace, before she leans in and kisses him. The scene from last night, his infidelity playing out in front of him.

Harper is sick. He can't take his eyes off of the screen. Someone has deliberately sent in this feed. His heart is pounding.

"Harp, Jessa was found last night strangled in her apartment."

Harper can feel the blood drain from his face. He can feel the bile and venom rising up in his chest. His Jessa, murdered. He feels lightheaded.

"Are you okay, Harper?"

"Yes. I just ... I'm all right."

Agent Walthrop says, "Harper, you know how this works. We're going to get the preliminary results back from Quantico soon. Anything you want to tell us about last night?"

Harper is tempted to get on a plane and oversee the operation himself. All of it, the fingerprints, the DNA, all of it would lead to him. Now that the FBI is involved, everything flows through them, and his office has very little control over it.

He is all too familiar with the process, an army of scientific experts and special agents working in a state-of-the-art facility in rural Virginia; they would provide a thorough forensic exam. They wouldn't miss a thing. He has a heavy heart from the news of Jessa, but the adrenaline has taken over his body. He knows he's in trouble.

Belle says, "This video was taken early evening, but the time of death was much later, around midnight. A neighbor found the key to the elevator still in the lock and entered the apartment to find Jessa dead. There were visible signs of strangulation. She put up a fight. Harper, we need to understand this video, and we need to know where you went after it was taken."

"Where did it come from?" Harper asks, as if in a trance.

"An anonymous remailer. Most likely Tor. We can't trace it back."

"Tor?" Detective Ganer says.

"Part of the dark web. It can host websites through its hidden services, sites like the Silk Road, the Internet's foremost open drug bazaar. You can buy and sell anything: guns, drugs, child porn, all online in exchange for bitcoins."

"In this case, Belle was directed to a random website and given a user name and a password. He had a few messages waiting for him there," Agent Walthrop says.

"A few?" Harper asks. He can't stop thinking about last night's fight with Seraphina and how it relates back to the clue from Brooke Beck's murder: *Heaven has no rage like love turned to hatred, Nor hell hath no fury like a woman scorned.*

Someone is setting him up, and he is playing right into it. Harper's mind is spinning. He needs to talk to Belle alone to figure out how deep this is.

"That's fine. I have nothing to hide. I went to see Jessa last night, just to talk to her, to see if I could get any more information about the other girls, the escorts that she worked with, to get a lead on Brooke Beck's case. I was comforting her, and it may have gotten a little physical. Seraphina and I have been having trouble lately, and I had an affair with Jessa Dante. I'm not proud of it. I left and went home. I can't believe she's dead." Harper says.

"We have no new information on the Renaissance Killer, but we know Jessa is connected to Brooke Beck and that they worked together. We got one more surprise e-mail addressed to you, Harp," says Agent Walthrop.

Harper opens the e-mail with apprehension. "Whatever satisfies the soul is truth. July 15, 1996."

Now Harper's body is tense with recognition. That quote from Walt Whitman and the date from his childhood still haunt him. It's a day he would rather forget.

"I grew up at the Walt Whitman Housing Project in Fort Greene. I was fifteen at the time, and it was the nineties. Guns and violence were just a part of the community. My father was a big, burly man, and he had a bad habit of hitting my mother when he was drunk. That night, a neighbor called to warn my mother about his agitation, and my intuition told me something bad was going to happen. He threatened to kill us both with a shotgun."

He looks at Belle, who nods, encouraging him to go on. "So I told my mother to lock the door to the bedroom, just like I always did, but that was when I heard him fire the first shot. I didn't give him the chance to fire a second one. I shot him with my own handgun."

"Did you ever face prosecution?" Walthrop says.

"I never faced prosecution because I was a kid and I acted in self-defense to protect my life and the life of my mother."

Belle nods, an acknowledgment of the pain and a story he must have heard a million times before.

"Everyone knows what happened with my father. It's an old story."

"Was anyone else there that night to witness what happened?" Agent Walthrop asks.

"Agent Walthrop, should I have a lawyer here?"

"We're just talking. I'm asking you if anyone else was there the night you shot your father, other than your mother, who is now deceased."

"No. It was just the three of us."

"It does demonstrate that you have a history of violence, and now it seems you've added violence against women to the list," Agent Walthrop says, looking at him with laser focus.

Belle can sense the growing tension and chimes in. "Harper, when I couldn't reach you on the phone, I tried the house and spoke to Seraphina. She said she was badly shaken after a violent fight with you. She said you hit her and she was bruised and her hand cut pretty badly. I asked her to come in so we could ask a few questions about last night," Belle says, avoiding Harper's piercing gaze.

"I went home, and Seraphina was acting crazy again. We started arguing. She threw my cell phone against the wall and shattered it. She blocked the door, and I pushed her to try to get by. She lost her balance and fell. It was just an accident."

"And where did you sleep?"

"In my car in the driveway."

"And did anyone see you sleeping in your car in the driveway?" Agent Walthrop asks.

"Agent Walthrop, are you married?" Harper says.

"I am."

"Then you know how it is. Things get heated."

"No, Swift, I don't know how it is. I do know that I've seen you on TV a lot lately, just sucking up the screen time. The camera loves you. It's like you think you're some sort of movie star or something," Walthrop says.

"I'm beginning to think you don't like me very much. I don't need to tell you that digital imaging is the easiest thing to manipulate. Creating pixels in a file is as easy as creating a document in Word. You can't really think I killed Jessa Dante and then beat up my wife? If so, prove it or stop wasting my time."

Belle drops his head, knowing this isn't going to go over well with Walthrop.

"I think I can trace all of this back to you, Harp. You were the last person to see Jessa Dante before she was brutally murdered. Your wife says you've been drinking a lot lately and staying out late partying. You father was a raging alcoholic who cheated on your mother every chance he got. Sounds like the apple didn't fall far from the tree."

"Why don't you find out where these e-mails are coming from?" Harper screams, fists curled and ready to fight.

"What happened before and after the video, Harp? And where were you at midnight?"

Agent Walthrop has a reputation as the playground bully. Harper always found it difficult to work with the FBI. A known rivalry existed between the FBI and Harper's work with the NYPD's Intelligence Division. There will always be tensions that flare up, given both agencies are made up of human beings.

Belle says, "We're working on it, Harp. This person is going to a great deal of trouble to stay anonymous."

Harper can see Seraphina through the glass window of his office; her left hand is bandaged. He thinks she has added a few more nicks and bruises. She is seated quietly in the reception area, looking like the poster child for domestic violence.

Harper is well aware of his wife and her flair for drama. Walthrop and Ganer agree to take a break, long enough for Belle to sit down with Seraphina.

As the door closes behind them, he clicks on the hyperlink and watches the video of Jessa. It's all he can do not to totally lose it. He has to compartmentalize or he will be frozen. He watches her move toward the camera, as if she's looking directly at him, lips moving, like she's trying to tell him something.

Harper zooms in on Jessa's face. The picture becomes grainy and pixelated but he can still see the fear in Jessa's eyes.

He thinks he can see her mouthing the words, "Help me."

Thirteen
SERAPHINA SWIFT

I am in a tiny room, staring across the table at Detective Belle.

"Seraphina, I know you and Harper have been having a hard time lately. I need to ask you a few questions about last night."

"I'm glad you asked me to come in. We've been friends for a long time, the three of us."

I knew from Harper that others would be observing through the other side of a two-way mirror. I had to be convincing.

Belle sighs, looks at his notepad, and says, "It's really important you stick to the facts about Harper, Seraphina. I know you have a rich imagination."

"Patrick, I haven't been sleeping well, and we've been fighting all the time. Lately, all I feel from him is anger. It's like he wants me dead. I keep seeing the same boat off our dock, and a stranger was watching me very late into the night. My mind may have been playing tricks on me, but I swear someone was just staring at me, and then my cell phone rang and nobody was on the line. The day I got into a car accident, someone was following me. I told Harper, but he doesn't believe me. My own husband doesn't believe me."

"Seraphina, you don't seem well. Your anxiety is off the charts, and you seem like you're in a manic state."

"Patrick, he's out every night, and now I find out he's been fucking another woman. How am I supposed to act when my family is falling apart? I'm home alone all of the time, and I'm afraid. I have to be able to protect myself and my child. For all I know, Harper could be the one trying to kill me."

"Seraphina, what motive could he possibly have to want to hurt you?"

"Everything we own is in my name. I paid for everything, all of it, with money from my family's estate. All of our assets belong to me. Last night, I found a book in his gym bag with the pages folded down. It was a crime novel about a man who murdered his wife and got away with it. I found sections highlighted and pages folded down. It's like he was researching how to get away with murder. I found a hotel receipt in his gym bag, and then I find him kissing another woman on a street corner. After last night, I really think he is the one that wants me dead, and I'm going to prove it."

"Look, I've known your husband for a long time, and it's hard for me to imagine that he would ever want to hurt you. He loves you very much."

My head is spinning.

"I know it sounds hard to believe, but I never thought my husband was capable of cheating on me either."

He slides a picture across the table. "Is this the woman you saw him kissing on the street corner?"

"Yes, that's her."

"And did you confront her?"

SEEING RED

I am choosing my words carefully, the panic rising within me.

"Jessa Dante was murdered last night. She was strangled in her apartment," he says, watching me closely.

"I went to see Jessa last night to confront her. I asked her to stay away from Harper for the sake of our daughter. If nothing else, we're still a family. It wasn't a violent situation."

"What happened to the lamp? The one that was broken and had your prints all over it."

My stomach tightens, and the heat rushes in; my cheeks flush with anxiety. My mind races, caught in the shock of this moment. When I left last night, I think Jessa was still breathing. I can still see her chest rise and fall as the doors of the elevator opened.

I was so angry. I was seeing red. At some point, I must have blacked out. I'm searching for the memories but I keep coming up with more blank spaces, just like that night in Boston.

I can't remember the rest. No matter how hard I try. Was I capable of murder?

I say calmly, "So, let's play that out. You think I attacked her and choked the life out of her. Do you really think I'm that strong? You can't think I had anything to do with this. Patrick, she was a paid escort. It could have been anyone. She could have liked rough sex. It could have been an accident. Some girls are into that sort of thing, you know."

"Look, your prints are all over the crime scene. We know you confronted Jessa and that you fought with her," he says.

"I didn't fight with her. She let me into her apartment by her own free will, and I asked her to stop sleeping with my husband because we have a child together. She's a woman. She understood and agreed to stop seeing him."

My mind flashes back to the lamp breaking and my rage at Jessa's advances. I can see her clearly lying dead on the floor, all beautiful and broken.

"I confronted Jessa, but I didn't stay. All we did was talk, and things may have gotten a little heated, but I didn't kill her. I'm not capable of that."

"Harper told me you've been struggling; the insomnia, the night terrors, and the paranoia. It must be awful for you, both of you, really. Is the medication helping at all?"

I can hear the beating of the steel drum inside my head, loud and throbbing, like a screaming train.

"Seraphina, Harper says you're acting crazy and that you blocked him from leaving after violently attacking him. I feel like you're not being honest, and I need for you tell me what the hell happened last night. Harper is in trouble."

My anger is building like a storm rising. I can no longer feel my breath.

"Last night, I saw my husband kissing another woman. I didn't even know her name until you just told it to me. I confronted her, but all we did was talk. She agreed to end the affair, and I left. That's the truth. Harper is the one who cheated. He is guilty. So why are you interrogating me? I'm just trying to keep my family together."

I start to cry now; the tears flow easily.

Belle lets out a deeper exhalation. He seems to deflate in his seat, the chair swallowing him up, and I'm alone in this tiny room.

"I went home, and Harper was drunk. I confronted him about Jessa. He threw a glass against the wall, and then he pushed me into the broken glass. He drinks all of the time now and never comes home. It's no secret his father was a raging alcoholic and a womanizer. He came at me, eyes blazing—like he wanted me dead."

"Harper says you lost your balance and you fell. He feels very bad about what happened," Belle says.

"Are you questioning whether or not I was attacked?"

"Yes. I am."

"And if I was a man? Would you still be questioning me?"

My anger is like a burning flame inside me.

"Do you really think Harper is capable of doing something like this?" he asks.

"I think my husband is brilliant and the only man I know who could get away with murder."

I can tell Belle is retreating. "Think about it. Do you really think he killed his father to protect his mother and that it was all self-defense? He's got anger issues. He's out of control. You just can't see it. He's charming, and he's got you fooled just like everybody else. I have no idea where he slept last night. I just know it wasn't with me."

I'm shaking now, and my hand is on the doorknob, my eyes stinging from holding back the tears.

"We're done here, Patrick. If you need any more information, you can go through my lawyer."

Now I know not all women are born warriors; some are molded through pain and suffering until they find the strength to break through their breakdown. I was the only one with enough mettle to face my husband and to hold him accountable for what he had done. After all, true love can't be found if it never existed, and ours burned so brightly, it could have melted the wings of Icarus.

I just set his truth in motion by smoking it out, separating it from all of the fiction.

Now he will be forced to swallow his pride, the taste of it, as bittersweet as his lies. I only needed thirty minutes with Detective Belle to paint a convincing picture of my husband as a psychopath.

I wouldn't allow him to turn the tables on me, making me out to be a jealous and unstable housewife, bored and unhappy with her lot in life. My marriage is my Bastille, very much like the prison in Paris. I have far too many grievances falling on deaf ears. Now that my husband has eaten her cake, bad blood flows and burns, molten hot like lava. It's still gleaming and glowing, long after the fire is out.

My phone is ringing, but I don't answer it. A minute later, it beeps to alert me that I've gotten a text from Harper. It's just three letters.

WTF?

I can see him, furious, clouds of smoke billowing from his ears like a Looney Tunes character. Moments later, the phone rings again, but this time it's my father calling me back.

"Hi, Dad. I can't talk right now."

"We spoke to Harper. He says your anxiety is acting up. I'm going to call in a prescription. You need to go back on your meds, honey. You know anxiety disorders run in the family."

"Thanks, Dad, and so does misogyny. Did they make a pill for that yet?"

"Do not go off your medication. You're a mother now, and you need to be healthy for your child. Harper says the nightmares are getting worse and you're acting crazy. Come in and I'll fix those dark circles under your eyes."

"Dad, stop taking his side all the time. I'm not crazy. I'm just not sleeping. I saw Harper with another woman. He's cheating on me."

I hang up on him. My father has never supported me, and he never will.

I leave a message for Jacob Akani, requesting to start Krav Maga training tomorrow. I will need more than words to defend myself if someone is out there and they come for me.

As I drive through the Lincoln Tunnel, the glow from the LED lights casts a strange glimmer on the faces as they flash by. At its deepest point, this tunnel is ninety-five feet underwater.

My mind plays tricks, a hallucination of water rushing in around me, cars bobbing, like apples in the rising tide, crushing me. I start to breathe, retreating to the safe corners of my mind, breathing in and out, using the tools Dr. Ellis has given me.

Like Alice, I feel like I have fallen down a most peculiar rabbit hole when I see the end of the tunnel. I put my foot on the gas, and I'm spit back out into the sunlight.

Fourteen
SERAPHINA

A psychopathic serial murderer doesn't end the violence after one horrifying kill but waits in the darkness, lurking in the shadows and looking for his next victim. He has no conscience or empathy. Often, there is no revealing confession. They are organized and intelligent, and often leave no trail of witnesses, fingerprints, or DNA.

I don't think my husband is a killer, although I made him out to be one. For me, fear has been replaced by a much more useful emotion: rage.

Most of the time, the killer is a stranger, one who's not motivated by revenge, jealousy, or greed.

I will not allow myself to be made a victim again.

Jacob is standing behind me, grasping the gun, which is smaller than I remember, more compact. He's wearing old faded Levi's and a black hoodie. He puts the earmuffs over my ears and hands me black glasses.

"If you are going to take a shot, it better be the one that kills," he says. "Are you nervous?"

"A little. I didn't grow up around guns."

"My father was a guard and weapons instructor at a maximum-security prison, and that made him view the world in a different way. I never learned to ride a bike. Instead, I learned to shoot in my backyard," Jacob says.

"What does it feel like when you pull the trigger?" I ask.

"Powerful. You need to focus on your breathing and staying calm. It will stabilize you so that you won't lose your balance from the recoil."

The sound of laughter floats in through the glass window and distracts me.

"Those are the 'guntry club girls' in the booth next to us."

"The what?" I ask.

"They come here every week instead of golf and call themselves 'the guntry club girls'. We've got Wi-Fi, comfy lounge chairs, a catered lunch, and they like to shoot. Take your finger off the trigger until you're ready to shoot. Focus and don't take your eyes off the target, and always point your gun downrange. You need to know your target and what's behind it."

He hits a button, and the target floats forward on a line.

"You can handle anything, Seraphina. It's about building confidence. When you draw your gun out there, you have to accept responsibility for someone dying. Watch me."

He lines up the gun and pulls the trigger, a clear shot through the center of the target.

A copy of the *New York Post* sits on a table in the other room. I can see Jessa's face on the cover, but I can't read the headlines. I'm distracted.

"A semiautomatic has a slide and is magazine fed. The slide racks back every time so you need a firm grip on the gun. Now you try." He hits the button, and a blank target comes into frame.

I point the gun. I'm distracted.

"This isn't a slow dance. Sometimes you only get one shot. Own the moment."

I line it up. I shoot straight down the middle. The recoil of the gun knocks me back a little at first. The gun goes up, and the shell is ejected, a feeling that will take some getting used to.

"How did it feel?" Jacob says.

"It feels like control and power. How long does it take to get really good?"

"It's muscle memory, like any other sport. You need to practice. If you come here every day for the next seven days and just practice, it can happen pretty quickly."

"What are my options to carry and conceal? And please don't show me anything pink."

Jacob laughs. "You have so many options."

"A purse carry?"

"You can't get to it fast enough, and what happens if someone steals your purse?"

"Inside the waistband?"

"I would go with the Flashbang Bra Holster."

"Are you serious?"

"Yes. You don't wear office clothes, and you're petite. Did I teach you how to rack the slide?" he says, smiling.

"Did you just say 'rack'?"

"I did. A semiautomatic pistol uses the energy generated by firing the first round to expel the spent casings and draw in the rest of the rounds from the magazine. The first round has to be chambered manually. That's called 'racking the slide.'"

"I'll get someone to help you with that holster, love. Keep practicing."

My mind wanders again. I lock eyes with Jacob. He has a look of curiosity mixed with concern.

"It's going to take some time. You just need to be patient."

I think about my child, my silver lining. Everything I do is for her.

Out the window, dark clouds move through the affluent shores of Rumson, the tranquil waters now dark and choppy.

It reminds me of my dream last night.

I was playing in the backyard with Sky, drawing a rainbow on the concrete in pastel-colored chalk. She was older, with beautiful golden curls spread down around her shoulders. She was laughing and jumping rope. The sun surrounded her, creating a golden halo. The laughter was like a melody. In the distance, I saw a tornado forming.

The wind whipped the clouds into a dark vortex of heavy gray smoke, violently twisting and turning, threatening to swallow us up.

I knew that wasn't right and that you couldn't have a bright day filled with sunshine and a tornado less than a hundred miles away, threatening devastation.

"Will you let me disappear?" Sky asked.

I tried to answer, but I had lost my voice. I couldn't move; my feet were frozen as if in cement.

"Mama, will you save me?"

She had the beautiful face of an angel. I still had no voice, and then Harper was there. He was just watching me, and they spoke in unison, all of us thrown into this macabre turmoil that the approaching violent tornado had created.

I tried to scream; the tornado ripped closer, destroying everything in its wake. Before I could grab Sky, she was caught up in it and vanishing into a black hole of destruction.

I woke up frightened and alone, made my way to the nursery, and slept on the rocking chair.

My mind is preoccupied now, working out the dream and its meaning. Jacob is still talking. I have faded away again. This must be what madness feels like.

"Seraphina, I know you're afraid. You're not alone. I'm here to help you. You're safe now. You have to keep moving forward. You can't keep holding on to what is already gone. You're not a victim. You're a survivor and a fighter."

"I can't remember what happened that night in Boston. I have no real memories of it. I just remember waking up in the hospital."

Then came my tears, tears that illuminated and revived; the same ones that had frozen around my heart began to melt and regenerate.

Jacob stayed with me, teaching me the proper stance and how to draw.

"You keep tightening your grip as you pull the trigger. See how you keep hitting the target too far down and to the right? Stay loose. You're tightening up. Keep breathing."

I shoot. The bullet pierces the bull's-eye.

"I think that's enough for today. You can come back tomorrow. Every day if it makes you feel better. For some people, this is an important part of recovery."

"Thanks, Jacob. I'll be back tomorrow morning."

At home, I walk through the rooms of the dark, quiet house. I feel alone and frightened, even with Birdie and Sky sleeping soundly down the hall; those pictures from Jessa's murder haunt me. Her smile, suspended in a wicked slant, mocks me, even in her demise.

Death is a demon, voracious and self-indulgent. It sounds an alarm deep in the soul, threatening the very core of our existence. It's gnawing away at our worst fears; it's a powerful sorcerer, planting the seeds of doubt and misfortune until they are soon overgrown weeds.

Is it my reflection I see in the vulture's eyes? The thought of it makes my blood run cold.

Fifteen
SERAPHINA AND HARPER

The flashbulbs go off around Harper. He feels the heavy weight of dread and fear, sitting like an anvil on his chest.

The headline of the *New York Post* reads, "Swift, Justice Served!" His heart is banging, rapid and hard; his jaw is clenched, pulse racing. This arrest wasn't anything he anticipated, but the evidence against him had been overwhelming.

Harper sits in the same interrogation room, this time on the other side of the table, as they interview him.

Overnight, someone had anonymously sent photographs of Harper and Jessa fighting from the night of the murder. The incriminating evidence makes him look like a madman who is one step away from wielding a scalpel and brutally murdering his girlfriend.

The photos show Harper grabbing Jessa roughly, Jessa fighting back, Jessa crawling toward him, and the whole sordid affair caught on film in black and white, like still shots from an old movie.

Scraping samples showed Harper's DNA was found under Jessa's fingernails, and his fingerprints were all over her apartment, along with his DNA on the swabs of the rape kit. It's as if someone had planned the perfect murder and set him up to be the killer.

He thought about Jessa mouthing the words *help me* on the video stream and realized someone had put her up to it. Harper could count his enemies on one hand, and none had the motivation to pull off a perfect crime like this.

Belle, ADA Kane and Agent Walthrop were waiting for him at the office that morning to break the news and brought him into the interrogation room.

After he listens intently to everything they have to say, Harper finally addresses the room. He says, "I admit to having an affair with Jessa, but do you really think I'm capable of murdering a woman like that?"

Agent Walthrop throws his hands up in a defensive gesture and says, "You want us to question whether or not you could actually commit a crime so heinous, right, Harp? Isn't that all part of your plan?"

Harper isn't afraid to invoke the Fifth. He knows he isn't guilty, and invoking his Fifth Amendment rights would keep him from doing any more damage answering these questions.

Agent Walthrop goes on, "I think you didn't realize your new girlfriend was a working girl, a paid escort. You had everything to lose, so you wanted to keep her quiet. She had all of the power. And judging from your financials, your wife owned you too. The truth would have cost you everything, and that's your motive," Walthrop says.

"We put a rush on the rest of the testing, including DNA. We should know more in a day or so," Belle says, obviously pissed at the turn of events.

Harper should have confided in Belle when the affair with Jessa first happened. They could have brainstormed, come up with a plan, and gotten out in front of all of this direct evidence.

"Did you find out where those anonymous e-mails came from or anything more on the murder of Brooke Beck?" Harper asks.

"Not yet," says Walthrop.

"Then you really don't have all of the answers yet, do you? I think you're embarrassed and need somebody to take the fall. I think you're setting me up. I had an affair with Jessa Dante, and that is all," Harper says.

"Harper Swift, you're under arrest for the murder of Jessa Dante," says ADA Kane.

They set the bail at $500,000. Harper pays and hires a lawyer, the best in the city. At first, he was furious at Seraphina. Her antics yesterday had cast a bigger spotlight around him as a prime suspect in the wake of Jessa's murder. He spent most of the night stewing, angry as hell at her. He knew forensics would turn up the heat on him and that there was enough direct evidence to incriminate him. He just didn't realize he would be thrown into the fire so quickly.

He goes over the steps in his mind, like he had been taught to do in any unsolved homicide case. Only this time, he is the suspect.

He remembers the clue from Brooke Beck's murder: *Heaven has no rage like love turned to hatred, Nor hell hath no fury like a woman scorned.*

Brooke Beck's murder led to his affair with Jessa, which led to Seraphina's rage after discovering his affair that night in SoHo.

It's as if someone is one step ahead of him, each move carefully planned and coordinated, as if his life has become a game of chess, the board springing to life, leaving him facing a loss and the ultimate death of his king.

He begins to wonder if Seraphina may have been telling the truth and whoever is after her is now taking revenge on him, carefully plotting and knocking him out of the equation with deception and lies.

He stays silent at the news conference, waiting for it to end so he can talk to Belle and a cybercrime specialist. He needs to figure out who is sending these e-mails. He needs to put the pieces together before it's too late.

Yao Lu is with computer forensics, a cybercrime specialist. She has bangs that hang down in front of her face and dark hair, with streaks of bleached-blonde at the ends. She wears a thick skull ring on her finger and scans the screen as her fingers dance across the keyboard.

"Can you tell me who sent this e-mail?" Belle asks.

She takes her headphones off and folds her delicate arms across her chest, rolling her chair over to another laptop open in the corner, Skrillex playing in the background.

"You don't get many personal e-mails do you, Belle?"

Despite his bad luck, this makes Harper laugh.

She says, "It's impossible to trace these. The links are useless, and the websites are hidden."

Belle looks at the white pieces of printed copy paper with lines of code.

"It came through the dark web, which bounces it all over the world before it ends up with you."

"How do we search the dark web?" Harper asks.

"Well, see, that's the thing. Without boring you with all of the computer jargon, you can't. The dark web is a section of the Internet not discoverable by conventional means, like Google or search or by directly entering a website URL."

"Why? Isn't it like Amazon, Facebook, or anything else that exists with an online address?"

"These websites are completely hidden; you can buy or sell anything because it's an underground marketplace. This looks like Tor. They disguise their web traffic to keep things anonymous."

"Is there anything we can do?"

"If I can access the computer server and run it from here, I can try to use a hacking tool, NIP network investigative technique, to uncover the IP addresses involved."

"How long will it take?"

"I'm not sure it's going to work. I may not be able to get around the encryption. You have to give me some time."

"Is this legal?" Harper says.

"It's controversial, but you're no stranger to controversy. I'm sorry, Harp. This could take months."

Harper stands up, stretching his arms up, trying to break up some of the knots in his back. The beat of the music is drilling a hole in his brain.

"Hey, can I turn this off?" Harper asks.

"Sure, old man," she says, smiling.

"Seems like someone is really trying to remain anonymous."

Yao says, "Now on Brooke Beck's computer, I was able to track her search history. She spent a lot of time on Internet detective sites, mostly researching the Renaissance Killer, the Boston serial killer. She's also been researching you, Harp. She seems to know everything about you."

"Why?"

"I thought maybe you could tell me."

"I was in law school at Harvard during the time of the Renaissance Killer and the Boston murders. I only know about them through the media reports and Seraphina. Did you get anything else off of the browser histories?"

"Those girls worked very hard. If you can call that work."

"What do you mean?" Harper asks.

"They both had very popular deep webcam sites."

"What is a deep webcam site?"

"You've never heard of Bate, where amateurs live stream erotic porn? They're tipped with tokens. It's a huge business. It looks like Jessa was ranked the third-most-popular porn website last year."

"Do they give awards for that?" Belle asks.

"The Cammies?" Yao says, laughing.

Harper isn't laughing. "Anything else we can do?"

"I installed software on both of your computers that allows me to monitor your activity and track your location from here. This way, if anything else comes in, we'll have it in real time. Just try not to watch too much porn, because I'll be watching you while you watch it," Yao says, trying to lighten the mood.

The thought of porn couldn't be further from his mind. Harper decides he will stay at Belle's apartment on his pullout couch for the night.

By now, the reporters will have camped outside his home, ruthlessly waiting for a glimpse into his demise.

He has sent extra security to the house to take care of Seraphina and Sky. He realizes his family is in danger, and he needs to put the pieces together before it is too late.

In the morning, he will apologize to Seraphina. He isn't sure she is done giving him the cold shoulder, punishing him for his infidelity. He still loves her, even more now that he realizes she isn't crazy—or maybe still crazy, but in the way that he has always loved her for.

The strange African poison used in the Boston murder makes the possibility of a serial killer very real.

Walthrop was a rising star with the FBI, having worked with NCAVC, the National Center for the Analysis of Violent Crime, a major branch of the FBI's Critical Incident Response Group. They investigate and research behavior of serial and violent criminal behavior. Serial killers and rapists are almost always male.

Harper says, "If the murders are connected, the killer needs to have the strength to move and cut these bodies. We can't rule out the possibility of a 'visionary' killer, given the ritual element to Brooke's murder. It doesn't fit the profile of a psychotic. He's organized and has managed to leave a trail of victims behind, if the Renaissance Killer and the Boston killer are related to Brooke Beck and Jessa Dante. I'm not sure what it all has to do with Seraphina and the night she was attacked.

"With this type of killing, there is very often a cooling-off period in between. And I think that explains the time between the murders now and what happened in Boston. Crimes like this are uncommon and often driven by sadistic compulsions."

"How about the secret society that Jessa told you about?" Belle asks.

"The Skull Club sounds like some benign conspiracy crew. This guy preys on women in the sex trade because they are often overlooked and forgotten. As for motivation, it could be religious or some fucked-up form of vigilante justice," Harper says.

"Have Lara circle back with Boston and pull everything on those murders. I need you to run an inquiry on a boat that Seraphina has seen off the dock of our house for the last few months. She feels like someone has been watching her and the baby. Also, she said she was followed the day of her car accident. Get the report."

"Jesus, Harp, you thought she was crazy. What if she's been right all along and someone is setting you up?"

Harper feels his head spin. He closes his eyes. He isn't sure how much more of this he can take before he uncovers the truth.

Sixteen

SERAPHINA

I wake early to an apologetic message from Harper. *I never meant for this to happen.* I don't know what type of evidence they have on him, but I know my husband. He is guilty of having sex with another woman, but not of committing a crime as hideous and gruesome as the murder of Jessa Dante.

Then I think about Harper, his history with his father and all of the drinking. Could he have murdered Jessa Dante? If so, who killed Brooke Beck and why?

Deep down, I want to believe Harper is innocent. I have to believe the father of my child is a good man, and his affair with Jessa Dante was a mistake and his only affair. That doesn't explain the anger I feel from him all the time now.

I feel like no marriage is safe from a woman like Jessa. I just have to find out who's behind all of this, and catch the predator as he spins his web of lies.

Harper is an easy target. He has an allegiance to pain, a foundation set from his childhood that is no longer permeable.

If only Harper believed in me from the beginning, we could have put an end to things before all of these events were so violently kicked into motion. The murderer is still out there, gaining strength and force, like a hurricane.

My memory is broken. The weight of my panic attacks is crushing me. The anniversary of my attack has passed, and my fears remain. I will learn to fight for the sake of my child, so she will have a voice. She is so innocent and peaceful as I watch her sleep in her crib, unaware of the danger that preys upon our family.

I drive straight to Jacob and practice shooting for hours. I have some basic skills from summer sleep-away camp and archery practice. It takes the same skill and precision to fire a gun and hit a target. I have natural talent. I'm now carrying the gun on my body. It takes me four seconds to draw and shoot it from the Flash Bang holster.

"That's too long," Jacob says. "You would be dead. You need to practice in the mirror when you go home tonight. I will time you again in the morning."

For the first time, I'm not stewing, mind racing and out of control. This must be how Harper feels all the time. He's always so unemotional and detached, just moving forward, one step at a time, never getting overly wrought or too far ahead.

I'm just sticking to the facts and working toward a goal, letting no obstacles stand in my way. I can feel my body start to change and get stronger. I'm less bloated from the lack of alcohol and pills. My mind is clear and lucid. I want to train, get stronger, mind and body.

This is the only thing that is within my control, given that I am at the center of the storm. Everything twists and turns around my movements. I can still feel someone tracking me, watching me, wherever I go.

My cell phone rings.

"Hi, Dr. Ellis. Thank you for calling."

"Hi, Seraphina. I'm sorry to hear about Harper and everything you're going through. What can I do to help?"

"I don't think I'm being paranoid, at least not anymore. I think I'm at the center of all of these murders. I think someone has been stalking me, and I think they're framing Harper to get him out of the picture."

"I understand how you feel. I think we should talk about your medication."

"I'm not crazy. I swear. Please believe me."

"How can I help you, Seraphina? I can see you're in pain."

"Is there any way to recover what happened that night in Boston when I was unconscious?" I ask.

"We can try hypnosis. It's an aid to psychotherapy because the hypnotic state might allow you to explore painful thoughts, feelings, and memories you might have hidden from your conscious mind. Sometimes it also helps to block the awareness of pain."

"Is there a downside?"

"There is a risk of creating false memories—usually the result of unintended suggestions by me. It's not usually used to treat dissociative disorders for that reason."

"What else? I can tell you don't like the idea, but what choice do I have?" I say.

"Well, you could experience the pain from the attack all over again. It may be too much for you, at a time when you are healing, finally getting stronger, and moving forward. I think it's too dangerous."

"I don't think I can handle that right now. Is there anything else I can do?"

"We can try EMDR."

"What is EMDR?" I ask.

"Eye movement desensitization and reprocessing. It's been effective in treating post-traumatic stress disorder. It doesn't rely on talk therapy or medications, which I know you are opposed to."

"Thank you, Dr. Ellis. I'm willing to try it." I hang up.

I close my eyes. I inhale. I exhale, focusing on the breath and staying calm. Then I pick up the phone and hit speaker, replaying Carter's message.

"Seraphina, it's Carter. It was great to hear from you. I'm in Montauk. Why don't you come out for a visit? It's forty-five minutes on the seaplane. I'll send it for you if you're interested. It's really beautiful out here this time of year. Call me."

I call Carter back. If anyone can connect the dots to the night I was attacked in Boston and whoever is stalking me now, it's him. I must have mentioned something or someone in the days that followed. Any small clue could trigger a memory that would help me figure out the past.

In my mind, I'm hunted and stalked, hands tied behind my back. The memories are stuck on fast-forward in my mind, silently creeping up on me.

These flashbacks pursue and haunt, refusing to end their reign of terror, wreaking havoc on everyone around me.

Seventeen
SERAPHINA AND JACOB AKANI

The news of Harper's arrest went out like shockwaves. The police have set up barricades blocking all of the entrances to get to our home. TV crews are lined up with vans and satellite feeds, sharply dressed anchors in front of their microphones, commenting on our family and the fate of Harper's future.

Helicopters fly overhead, getting an aerial shot of the property. How ironic. I no longer feel alone.

A team of investigators, medical examiners and forensics investigators are going through our home, searching for evidence.

Harper texts me:

Where are you?

Fifteen seconds later, I reply:

I'VE BEEN CALLING YOU!

And then another from Harper:

I'M SORRY!

Please meet me at the Greenwich Inn at 7pm?

I don't respond. I let him feel the pain of having a partner quit, simply disappear like a missing person.

Still, even after his arrest and being out on bail, he does not come home. The one place he might find family, love, and some sort of redemption. It makes it harder for me to forgive his affair with Jessa. I've lost faith in our marriage, and I don't trust him anymore.

I get into the car, ignoring the onslaught of questions from meddling reporters, and slam the door, throwing it into reverse, speeding out, and leaving a trail of gravel and sand.

I head north on the Garden State, heading toward Jacob Akani. I have a plan, and I'm prepared to go at it alone. The clouds have rolled in, bloated and gray. My eyes are bloodshot, head pounding; I clench my hands tightly around the steering wheel.

I'm so tired, it's as if the entire world is on fire around me, the streets blazing, and everywhere I go, I leave a trail of ash and smoke in my wake. I've always been a magnet for destruction, the heat somewhere inside me, glowing and burning, like a heart on fire.

The air is heavy around me, as if the molecules stack up and exert pressure on my bones; so much pressure, it feels like they are about to break.

The weight of the barometric pressure rises all around me.

I manage to find a parking spot less than a block away from Jacob Akani, which is nothing short of a miracle or an act of God. I'm ready to start my Krav Maga training.

Jacob buzzes me in.

I step through the door, and the blare from the television distracts me. The local news is playing, and the anchor is abruptly laying out the murders, spinning her own bed of lies, with Harper now the scapegoat of the scandal as it unfolds.

Jacob turns off the television.

"Is it true? Is Harper guilty?" Jacob asks.

"He's guilty of being selfish and fucking another woman, but that's all. He slept with Jessa Dante on the night of the murder. I believe that is all he's guilty of. But right now, that's enough for me."

"Are you okay?" Jacob asks.

"I think one person is behind all of this. The killer was there the night I was attacked in Boston. And now they're after me. They just want Harper out of the way."

"Is that what you believe?"

"Yes, that is what my intuition tells me. I have a visceral feeling of being stalked. Mostly in my home, I have a very bad feeling that someone or something is watching me and my child all the time. I have shut down the part of me that has been questioning it, blaming it on my imagination, paranoia, or too much time on my hands. Whatever happened that night in Boston is coming back to haunt my family, and I need to fight to protect my child."

I take my gun out and put it on the table in between us. Somehow, it doesn't matter if I'm wrong, if all of this drama, the gossamer web I have spun, is somehow only in my mind, opalescent, a kaleidoscope of color.

My years with Harper have done irreparable damage, but I have emerged a warrior, one who is ready for the fight—and to win.

"Seraphina, when you are out on the street and you draw your gun, know that you accept responsibility for someone dying."

"I understand."

"Say it back to me."

"If I draw my gun, I accept responsibility for someone dying."

"That's good. Are you sure you're ready to start training? Are you present and committed?"

"I am present and committed. I will no longer live in fear. The next person that gets hurt will not be me. I have a child to protect. Please tell me you can help and give me enough skill quickly so that I can defend myself from another attack."

My skin feels hot and flushed, hands clenched, and it is hard to stop my legs from shaking.

I let the adrenaline course through me, resurrect me, rising up from the ashes, to bury a past that still haunts me.

"I can," Jacob says.

"Do you believe me?" I ask.

"Does it matter?"

I hear the beat of the drum again, this time getting louder.

"Tell me about the night you were attacked," he says.

"I don't remember much. Everything happened in slow motion. I couldn't think straight or hear anything but the voice of my attacker. I froze. And now I keep seeing that look of rage and his blue eyes. I was hit with something heavy, like a baseball bat, and then I blacked out."

"I'm sorry. That sounds like a terrifying, violent, and stressful encounter and one that you didn't deserve. No one has the right to invade your space or attack you in any way, mentally or physically. Repeat after me."

"No one has the right to invade my space or attack me in any way, mentally or physically."

"The feelings and thoughts you experienced during the attack are normal responses to a violent encounter. Trauma has a universal effect on the mind and body."

"What do you mean by normal response? You mean instinct?" I ask.

"Exactly. The first thing you describe is called 'speed of mind.' Even though it felt like slow motion, your mind was actually in overdrive, just processing at a more rapid pace."

He touches me lightly on the shoulder and says, "The second feeling you describe is 'tunnel vision,' and it's your body going into survival mode, focusing everything on the immediate threat. Soldiers on a battlefield experience it. You shouldn't have had to. The 'freeze' that you describe, that's just the brain shutting down, refusing to acknowledge the imminent danger."

"If these are all natural reactions or instincts, I need you to train me and replace them with the instincts of a killer."

"I can't do that. They're hard-wired because you're not a killer. We can do stress drills, but you have to be able to hear and process the information, stay present while still moving forward to deal with the threat. Keep breathing and visualize winning. You can't quit, and you can't disconnect. You have to push through, but I can't get rid of those instincts, and I can't promise you it won't happen again," Jacob says.

"I understand."

We warm up with shadow boxing, moving around the floor like a dance, ending up in fighting stance.

"What are the vulnerable targets?" Jacob asks.

"Eyes, ears, throat, and groin."

"Also, the kidneys, liver, and fingers. And when he hit you, did you fall to the ground?"

My mind goes back to that night, and I can see myself tumbling into the street. A car grinds to a halt. A second later, it would have crushed my skull. I remember begging for help as he drove around me, as if I were an obstacle standing in the way, as if all that mattered was getting on with his night.

"Yes."

"If that happens, protect your head and tailbone and always keep your feet between you and your attacker. You are vulnerable in that position, so get off the ground as soon as possible."

SEEING RED

Suddenly, I think of Jessa. I can see her so clearly on the ground, those bright-blue sapphire eyes gazing up at me.

"Don't let me hit you." He slaps me in the face, jolting me to present.

I push myself to stay focused. We work on more drills. I weave in and out.

"Focus on my voice, Seraphina. Keep breathing." He gives me black leather strike gloves.

"He can drop you with one good hit because he's stronger. You have to keep moving. You have to stay with me, Seraphina. You can move faster because you're lighter. And you're smarter. He won't expect you to fight back."

"Why do you keep saying my name?"

"Because I can see you disconnecting. Stop training and sit for a minute," Jacob says.

I sit on the mat, collecting my thoughts and my breath.

"Listen, I've worked with survivors like you, soldiers with more trauma than you can even imagine. Violence against women is a global pandemic, most of the time by an intimate partner. So, yes, I believe you're in trouble. I never doubted that. But hear me now: you are one of the lucky ones. You survived, and now you know you have a weakness. And it's not that you're a woman. You are human. You froze. You didn't fight back. Forgive yourself. You didn't know how to fight. Seraphina, that feeling of being a victim is etched in your mind, and you're the only one that can overcome it."

Then I can't stop the tears; my body feels battered and bruised, as if I have been pushed off the edge of a cliff, and the wounds are still bloody and bruised, only now, I'm bleeding on the inside. I feel like a zombie. None of this seems fair, and I let myself wallow in self-pity.

He takes me in his arms, exposing all of the scars I hide, until I've used up all of my tears, and the only thing left to do is fight.

"I was with the special unit, Israeli Defense Forces, for ten years. I've trained the counterterrorism unit. I have seen and heard it all. Unimaginable evil. I can give you the street-fighting skills you need, but you have to trust me. You can't keep overthinking this or letting your flashbacks and triggers interfere with training."

"Why should I trust you?"

"You can't trust your husband, and you think you're in trouble, right? So what choice do you have? Dr. Ellis sent you here because combat training helps with recovery. I can't walk with you. Once you leave through that door, you have to believe you can own the moment and that you can fight to win. You may only get one chance, so make it the best one you've got, have faith, and make your own truth."

I think about Brooke and Jessa. If they fought back, would they still be alive? Jacob is right. I couldn't have killed anyone. I don't have any idea how to fight back and win.

"I understand," I say.

"The most important thing is to stay calm. If you let fear take over, you lose. Visualize your opponent. Try to anticipate his next move. Make him swing more and miss. That uses up energy; let gravity and the energy around you help take him down."

My heart is pounding again. I can almost hear the voice of the animal that is pursuing me. He is potent, insatiable and devious.

"How many rounds do you have loaded?"

"Six plus one."

"Good."

"What do you do if he is choking you?" Jacob asks.

"I strike at his eyes."

Jacob says, "That's right, and use the same motion as Superman ripping off his shirt, up and out, sending your elbow into his face. You will need to think fast. Counter with something that will do the most damage or just cause enough pain to distract him, and then strike again until you win."

I can shut out the past. I will keep moving forward. I am getting stronger.

Jacob says, "A warrior's strength is measured by his capacity to empathize and forgive. You will be able to stand up in the face of adversity for the ones you love. You are stronger than you give yourself credit for."

Hope is the only thing that conquers fear. I am completely focused. My mind is open, and I will train to the point of exhaustion.

"Trust me: with three intense days of training, you will leave with enough skill to feel safe in your mind, out in the world, and in your own home. Nobody should have to live in fear. You have a family to protect."

I think of Harper and Sky. He's right. I need to see Harper.

We have so much damage between us, it's hard to know if we're broken beyond repair, shooting arrows at each other and striking at the heart.

If Harper is truly sorry, he will have to let me go, at least long enough to find the killer.

Eighteen
HARPER AND SERAPHINA

Gravitation is a natural phenomenon, the force of attraction that draws together any two objects in the universe. Our love has always been magnetic, and now I find myself pacing outside the Greenwich Hotel with its vermillion tapestry, trying to control the unseen forces that keep trying to rip us apart.

Even after Jessa and all that Harper has put me through, a part of me still wants him. When I see him walking toward me, looking tired and broken, my heart breaks with him. The strength of our love is still bonded by history and a child, and I have to fight for my own peace if I want to close the gap between us.

We walk through Locande Verde, getting lost in the rustic and industrial vibe and buzz of conversation swirling around us.

Harper is wearing a baseball hat, jeans, and a dark hoodie. We blend in and make our way into the lobby, where the breathtaking design, woodsy scent, and a shot of tequila soothe my nerves like Novocain.

We let the silence surround us, taking comfort in each other. I close my eyes for a moment and let the feeling of being safe surround me, that feeling of being alive and in this moment.

"You look like shit, Harp."

"I'm sorry. I should have trusted you. I didn't believe you. Can you forgive me?" Harper says.

"I don't know what to believe anymore or who to trust. All I know is our family is in trouble and I can't wait around for someone to save me."

He waits, knowing me and that I won't let him off that easily.

"I think I can forgive you for the affair, but not for doubting me. If you had believed me, none of this would have ever happened. We took an oath: in sickness and in health. Does that mean nothing to you?"

"It means everything to me."

"I was alone with Sky. I needed you. You left me alone, carrying the weight of all of it. You were out every day and every night."

He waits, looking deep into me, taking in every word. "And what I'm doing, raising our child, is just as important, and it's all right if nobody else sees it that way. But not you. You were supposed to get it. So when did you stop believing in me and start doubting us?"

"I'm sorry, but everything I've done is for us, our family. And your anger, it's like a fire that burns through everything. It's explosive, and I can't talk to you."

"I've always been that way, and you've always been able to take that kind of heat. You're my husband, my partner. You came into this with eyes open. I haven't changed. What kind of person turns away when someone they love is in need? How do you expect me to trust you and for us to have a future?"

"You pushed me away."

"I'm sorry for that. I really am."

Harper says, "I wish I could go back in time and do it all over again, but I can't. I know that I still love you, and I don't want to lose you. What more can I do? I miss you all the time. I know I fucked up. I'll spend the rest of our lives making it up to you. But the kind of love we have is rare, and I'll do whatever it takes to get you back."

He has tears in his eyes. "What can I do now to save our family?"

"Believe in me now. That is how you can support me and build back my trust. You cheated on me, Harp. I'm not sure if I can forgive you. I know our family is in danger."

"Where are you going?"

"I've learned how to shoot a 9-mm Glock. I'm wearing it now. I've been learning Krav Maga, so next time I find myself alone in a dark alley, I won't be the victim."

"I think it's too dangerous."

"I don't care what you think. It's too late for your opinion about this to matter. I feel I'm facing life and death, and I want to live. Finally, I want to live."

In his eyes, I see something I haven't seen for a long time: his fear and pain.

"I need you to take care of our daughter, get to know her, because she's amazing, and right now, she's the best thing about the two of us, if there even is an 'us.'"

I can see Harper visibly flinch, as if I have punched him in the stomach.

"I'm going to put my life back together so I can be a mother to my child. That's really all I ever wanted to be."

Harper says, "I never stopped loving you. And I never will."

As I walk away, I can feel my spirit, and with it a new light. I remember the lines and colors of the phoenix I painted, and I can see it now, rising up from a bed of lies.

SEEING RED

All of these years, banging my head against a wall, as I walk out into the darkness, spilling onto Greenwich Street, I find the strength that I have always been looking for. With each step, I grow stronger, the cobblestone streets of Tribeca stretching out underneath me.

Nineteen
SERAPHINA AND JACOB

I spend the weekend with Jacob, reenacting the attack and preparing myself for another violent encounter. Jacob pushes, to the point of breaking me in half. Stress drills, counterattacking strategies, targeted strikes to vulnerable points, and maintaining awareness of my surroundings, these are things that matter most in the case of another attack.

I call home to check on Sky. The sound of her voice brings tears to my eyes.

Now I feel like I need to keep pushing, train to get stronger, and blow off a little steam. I need to be alone, to think about everything, including Harper and last night's conversation.

As I enter Central Park, I'm struck by the dramatic view of the Manhattan skyline.

I decide to go for a run around the reservoir, which used to be one of my favorite things to do when we lived in the city. I lose myself in the pounding of my feet as they hit the soft surface of the dirt road, kicking up smoke. The fresh air and sweeping views of the park revive me.

It is a warm day, and the city is quiet. Memorial Day weekend is just on the horizon, unfolding into the start of summer. I lose myself in the rhythm of my surroundings.

My mind is clear and ready, and it doesn't take long for me to realize that someone is following me, tracking my every move. I test it by veering off onto another trail. This evil presence follows me, without breaking stride.

My senses heightened and on alert, I fight that feeling of regret, questioning my decision to venture out alone. I focus on the moment, staying calm and breathing, sharp and focused. No more regrets. If this is my moment, I own it.

I have no one to blame but myself for this decision. I haven't seen anyone else nearby since I came around the last bend. I scan for joggers, anyone to give me some sense of safety. It's all quiet. I'm alone with my thoughts.

In the distance, the sun is setting in shades of glowing amber. I can feel my heart rate accelerating, the increased speed and strength in my limbs as I run faster.

For a moment, doubt creeps in, and I wonder if this is all in my mind, but the training has conditioned me to trust the instinct that I am in danger.

Someone is stalking me.

I trip over a rock; the stress from the rising fear makes me lose some of my fine motor skills.

I can hear Jacob's voice in my head: "Remain calm. Keep breathing. Don't let the fear take over."

This is hard. The pain from my past is coming back to haunt me. That fear alone is powerful and hungry, like a wolf circling, threatening to devour me. I feel the outline of my gun. I am down to a two-second draw. This gives me comfort. I have the maximum number of rounds in the chamber.

I reach and draw the gun, turning to face my attacker. But nothing is there. I don't see a fierce man or beast.

All I hear are the faint sounds of nature and the whistle of the breeze as it gently shakes the leaves.

Nobody is on this path but me. It's dangerously quiet, and it's getting late. I veer off onto another path I think leads out of the park.

I think of the Robert Frost poem, "Two roads diverged in a yellow wood. I took the one less traveled by, and that has made all the difference."

I can't find my way out, and I'm alone.

I picked the wrong path, and it takes me around another winding bend, the quickest one out of the park and back into plain sight.

I put the gun away, realizing I'm in Central Park and I just took out my weapon. It must be my mind playing tricks after all. I convince myself it's just me, out here all alone.

I run faster. The path sweeps underneath a bridge, dark and twisty. I stop and listen. I look for a way around it, even if it means running up a hill, cutting through poison ivy, or climbing a tree. Anything is better than the dark path inside that tunnel.

Finally seeing no way around it, I edge forward, my face ashen and pallid. My hands are clammy, my legs weakening.

As I move through it, I hear a branch snap behind me. I run quickly through the tunnel and out into the sunlight. I stop on the other side and turn to look back, and another runner shoots by me, focusing only on his own race and getting to the finish line.

Then I'm alone again.

I focus on my breath. Easy. In and out.

SEEING RED

The clouds have rolled in on a wave of my anxiety. I wish it away, imagining it rises up above the clouds on wings of pixie dust and sand.

I see a path winding up and out of the park, and I change course. I take a few more slow breaths. I am tired of running.

In that moment, I don't see him as he steps out of the tunnel and grabs me by the hair, drawing me back inside the darkness.

At first I don't fight back; I let him pull me backward.

I can hear Jacob's voice in my head: "Stay calm. You know what to do. Breathe. Stay present."

My heart racing, I move my hands back as far as I can, with force, remembering the Superman motion, plucking his hands straight down, bringing my elbows to my sides.

I step back and send an elbow into his face as hard as I can, turning toward him.

He's wearing a black mask and I continue striking until he retreats and falls to the ground.

That's when I hear a familiar voice. "Seraphina. You can stop now. It's me, Jacob. I think you broke my nose."

I tear off his mask.

"Are you crazy? I could have shot and killed you."

"I know. But I'm wearing a bulletproof vest, and I taught you to aim for the heart. So really, it was a calculated risk," Jacob says, taking me in his arms. "I'm sorry."

We stand in silence, holding each other, my heart still pounding inside my chest.

Jacob wraps his arms around me tighter. I look up into his eyes, and they are blurred by violence and the depth of his emotions.

He turns me so I'm facing away from him and says, "I need to know that when you leave tomorrow, you will have the skills to defend yourself."

"Haven't I been tested enough? You didn't have to do that. I'm ready," I say.

"I didn't do it for you," he says.

Jacob kisses my hair softly, taking a deep breath in, both of us intoxicated by the undeniable thrill of his chase.

That night, I dream of Jacob, and I'm filled with love and desire for him. The streets are crowded and charged with erotic energy. We enter a movie theater, and I stumble through the darkness.

In front of me, I can see two rooms, one covered by a curtain of white light. I look inside and watch as Jacob and I make love.

Twenty
SERAPHINA AND CARTER

"**H**ave you ever taken off from the water?" the pilot asks.

"Never," I say, fastening my seat belt, safely in Carter's private seaplane, taking me to Montauk.

As the sun stretches out over the East River, the water sparkles and shimmers, like a treasure chest filled with gold. Soon we are up and soaring above it all, the water smooth as glass, a peaceful quiet place that calms the unrest churning deep inside me.

This view is infinitely better than the one from the Long Island Expressway, with droves of Manhattanites sardined along the highway, making the pilgrimage "out east" for the first big summer weekend in the Hamptons.

I will always love Montauk, the low-key cousin of the Hamptons, with its jewel-toned sunsets, high sand dunes, and beaches populated with wispy American beach grass.

Yesterday with Jacob, although terrifying, demonstrated his perversity—and an undeniable attraction growing between us.

Was I also intoxicated by the thrill of his chase? That rush of adrenaline and the power that comes from fighting back is turning into a twisted desire. The roles of teacher and student have always been precarious for me. Something inside me is drawn to darkness, chaos, and self-immolation, and now I have to fight the temptation of another vice.

As I step off the Cessna, my mood lifts, and I wonder about Carter. It feels good to be out of the city and away from the media circus that our lives have become.

Again I'm reminded of my first summer in Montauk with Harper.

I am positive Carter will show up with his car and driver. I squint and put my hand to my forehead for shade. I can see him by the curb now, just waiting.

I remember the last time we saw each other in Cambridge. He was angry that I was leaving. He had asked me to travel the world with him, just commit to a life of adventure and learning.

I wasn't ready for it at the time. It just wasn't the life I saw for myself.

For Carter, life was easy. He never had to work for anything. His family money left him spoiled and unwilling to accept anything less than the best of what life has to offer.

"Hi, beautiful. Look at you. It's great to see you." He stands there for a moment, gazing at me, taking in every detail.

"You too. I mean, you look great," I say, hugging him and letting him pull me close.

"I have a surprise for you," he says.

Carter has an easy, breezy style about him, dressed in colored chinos and a Ralph Lauren oxford with driving moccasins and sunglasses. He fits in perfectly, very Hamptons chic.

"I'm not sure I want any more surprises," I say.

He opens the door, and I climb into the back of the SUV.

Carter is still rugged and handsome. For a moment, I feel like I'm back at school, hooking up in the stacks of Widener Library.

"I'm sorry to hear about everything you're going through, and you know I'm here for you," Carter says. "I'm always here for you."

"Thank you. That's part of the reason I'm here. I want to talk to you about what happened in Boston."

"I know. I got your message. I thought it might be nice to go to Deep Hollow Ranch, and then we can talk over lunch. It's such a nice day, and I'm sure you need a break. Horseback riding always used to clear your mind. Do you still like to ride?"

"I do. That sounds great, but I didn't bring anything to wear," I say.

"I've got everything here. I had my assistant pick up some clothing and riding gear. I hope that's all right. Maybe we can take a tour of part of the former Warhol estate if you like," Carter says.

"That would be amazing. I have always wanted to see that estate. I've only seen it in pictures, that collection of white cottages overlooking the ocean and those sweeping views. It looks incredible. So many of my idols have passed through that estate—Jackie O., Lee Radziwill, the Rolling Stones, Truman Capote."

It feels so easy to be back with Carter. I never have to worry about anything. He takes care of it all.

I say, "Isn't it next to Peter Beard's house? My father is a collector of the End of the Game series, when he lived in Africa and documented the elephants and wildlife. Amazing stuff."

"I didn't know your father collected photography. I spent two years in Africa studying traditional African medicine."

"Really?"

"Yes, I sent you a letter. Did you ever get it?"

"No, I never got anything from you."

"Well, I did."

"I'm sorry. I would have written you back. I never got it."

"Nothing really. It's no big deal. Peter Beard was Warhol's crazy next-door neighbor. Rumor has it that he used to cut himself and paint in his own blood."

Carter adds, "And that he jumped in and out of a snake pit in his own home just to keep things interesting. I can show you his property. It's high up on the bluff."

He takes out a bottle of chilled rosé, opens it, and hands me a glass. It's strikingly pale in color, and I breathe in the aroma, fresh and fruity. It reminds me of summer.

"You remembered," I say. "Although I'm not sure I should drink and ride." We both laugh.

"You've gotten old. I remember the Seraphina from our wild college days. You were always up for anything."

He pours me a glass. "To us."

We clink glasses. I can't help but think, *There really is no "us."*

He notices my discomfort and changes the subject back to safe ground. "Can you believe Andy Warhol and Paul Morrissey bought that estate in the '70s for $220,000 and it recently sold for fifty million?"

"The insane world of Hamptons luxury real estate. That really is incredible. So, do you miss Boston and living in Back Bay? It was always so charming," I say.

"No, I love it out here. Have you been lately?"

"Not since the baby was born. Harper has been really busy at work, and it's just harder to get away."

"You had a little girl, right?"

"How did you know?"

"I keep up," he says with a mischievous smile.

"How about you? Did you ever marry?"

"Almost, but I just couldn't pull the trigger."

We arrive, driving past the wooden fence of Deep Hollow Ranch. The sign above it reads Oldest Cattle Ranch in the United States of America.

"This is breathtaking," I say.

I watch the waves break along the shoreline, pure kinetic energy; the force of it curves and slopes.

My horse is gentle and elegant. We spend the afternoon leisurely riding along the wooded trails, ending our ride, trotting on the beach, white pristine sand with crystal-clear water. The ride is breathtaking, a mixture of open fields and bluffs.

We pass Oyster Pond; its majestic beauty and grace open up to us. We see rabbits and turtles, taking me far from the city and all of my nightmares.

"This all seems like a dream," I say to Carter. "It's almost too good to be true. I never want to leave."

"Then don't. Stay with me for a while. Just until things settle down."

"I can't do that. I have to get back to Sky."

"Well, you're always welcome. Next time bring her with you. I would love to meet the mini Seraphina. She must be a real force, strong and beautiful, just like her mother."

He gazes into my eyes, letting them rest on my lips. "Are you hungry? he asks, looking me over as if to say I'm too thin.

"Yes, I'm starving."

"I know the perfect place. I thought we would have lunch at my house. I brought in lobster rolls from Gosman's Dock."

"That's my favorite. How did you know?"

"I didn't. Can't it be my favorite? Did you know Mick Jagger smashed his hand through the window at Gosman's and had to have twenty stitches?"

"No, I didn't," I say.

"I wonder what Bianca did to make him so angry," Carter says.

"How do you know it was Bianca's fault? Maybe he just didn't want a lobster roll," I say, feeling the effects of a second glass of wine on an empty stomach.

I plant my hands in my lap, lost, thinking of Sky and Harper and wondering how I got here, feeling like I'm on a date in Montauk.

"What just happened?" he asks.

"I need to ask you about Boston. For the past year, I've been feeling like someone is watching me. I keep seeing the same blue eyes in my nightmares. I can't eat. I can't sleep. I don't think I'm capable of killing the man who attacked me in Boston. I blacked out. I remember picking up the broken bottle, and then I was knocked unconscious by something heavy, like a baseball bat. I feel like someone else was there that night and that same person is stalking me. I know it sounds insane. I feel like they are behind all of this with Harper."

"I thought Harper had an affair."

"He did, but I think someone set him up."

"Why do you keep making excuses for him? Seraphina, you were always too good for him. You deserve better."

"Like you, Carter?" We sit in silence. My anger bubbles up, rising to the surface.

Carter says sweetly, "Yes, exactly. Like me. I always did love that fire in you. Listen, I don't want to fight with you. I think it's horrible what he's done. You have a child together, and you have given him everything. You didn't tell me anything about that night. You couldn't remember. Did you know Harper was at the bar that night?"

"No."

"Ask him. He was there. He had on a costume. I think he was dressed as the angel of death. I can't remember; it was so long ago. I saw him with his mask off at the bar."

SEEING RED

"After all of this with Jessa Dante, doesn't it make you wonder if maybe your husband is behind all of this, and maybe he's the one that's been stalking you? He's always had anger issues. You know he killed his own father. He's a cold-blooded murderer, and I think you are in danger."

"Harper's father was a drunk and cheated on his mother. He killed his father to protect his mother."

"Seraphina, you are being naive. He's out every night drinking, and you have proof that he's had an affair."

Carter's beach house is incredible. It is set back on the water, with a modern, contemporary design, and surrounded by sweeping views of the water. Carter takes me through the spa-style pool house, fully equipped with a steam shower and sauna, but my mind is spinning. All I can think about is Harper and finding out the truth.

I see a copy of the *New York Post* is crumpled up next to me, asking the question on everyone's mind. I pick it up and read it out loud: "Is Harper Swift Guilty?"

Now all I can think about is getting back to New York. I need to talk to Harper.

"I'm sorry, Carter. I think I need to get back to the city. I need to talk to Harper."

"I understand. I'll call the pilot and let him know you're ready to go back. You know I'm here for you. I can protect you. I will take care of you."

"I don't think I ever thanked you for taking care of me after the attack. You've always been there for me, Carter. I'm just not sure who I can trust. My family is in danger."

If there is any truth to what Carter is saying, I will attack Harper. I will go to the police and have him locked away in prison for years.

At this point, I'm not sure who I can trust or what to believe.

Twenty One
HARPER AND SERAPHINA

"**I**'ve been calling you all morning. Where have you been?" Harper asks me immediately as I walk through the door of Yao Lu's office.

Harper looks like he hasn't slept all night. He is standing with Detective Belle, ADA Lara Kane, and another man, someone I don't know, who is extending his hand toward me.

"Hi, I'm Agent Walthrop with the FBI, and this is Yao Lu, our cybercrime specialist."

"Hi everyone, and sorry, it looks like I'm late to the party. I was in Montauk visiting an old friend. I don't get much cell reception out there," I say.

"Carter?" Harper says, raising an eyebrow with an angry look on his face.

"Yes. Can I talk to you alone?" I ask.

"No. I need you to sit down and promise me that you're going to stay calm," Harper says.

"I can't promise you that, Harp. You seem to have a talent for pissing me off lately," I say. "But I'll try."

He sighs.

"The security system in our house has been hacked, including the camera, and that includes the baby's monitor," Harper says.

Now I remind myself to stay calm and keep breathing. "After I saw you last night, I went back home to check on Sky. I couldn't sleep. It was late, after midnight, and I walked by the baby's room. That was when I heard a voice, a man's voice, whispering. It was dark, and when I looked inside the room, I saw that it was coming through the monitor."

"What was the voice saying?" I ask, my voice steady and controlled.

Harper takes my hand, and in his eyes, I can see terror.

"What? You are scaring me. Just tell me," I say, raising my voice.

He plays the recording back from his cell phone.

The same terrifying whisper from that night in Boston fills the air around me, electrifying it.

The voice says, "Hickory dickory dock, the mouse ran up the clock."

I cover my mouth with my hands to stifle a scream, and then I can't hold back the tears.

My mind is spinning, and I'm terrified, my worst fears imagined.

"Seraphina, can you describe the man who came to your house that night?" Belle asks.

"He had jet-black hair. He smelled like a combination of hair dye and stale cigarettes. I couldn't really see his eyes. He wouldn't really look at me. Something seemed off about him, but then I never did anything about it."

"Were you drinking again? Don't you think you should have called me if you felt threatened?" Harper snaps.

"Really, Harp? Would you have answered or just let it go to voicemail because you were too busy 'working'?"

I close my eyes tightly and take a deep breath in. I feel anxious. The pressure is building again. That night, I thought I was paranoid, just my imagination on overdrive, but the danger was real.

"Sit down, Seraphina," Belle says. "Someone could be controlling the camera remotely, but we don't think so. You have a wireless camera, which sends video to a nearby monitor, where you can view it on your phone."

My heart is beating faster.

Belle says, "But some cameras transmit these images hundreds of yards, broadcasting them outside of the home, so anyone can pick them up by radio frequency or public airwaves. The signal can reach as far as five hundred yards away."

"Jesus, Harper. Did you get an ID on that boat that was so close to our house? Did you take out the hacked system? What have you done?"

I think about Sky. Is she safe now? Does she need more protection? Is she safe now?

I am panicking. The horror is beyond anything I can ever imagine. The vulture is still circling our family from above, and I feel helpless, unable to find a way to stop it.

"Yes, we're installing a hardwired system today. We've upgraded the entire thing."

I turn to Harper. "Where did you find these people? The ones who installed the system?"

"What? I was going to ask you that question. Remember, you found them online?"

Now Harper is looking at me, again like I'm crazy. "No. They canceled that day on my voicemail. That's why I was surprised when I got home and Birdie told me a new company had been by to install the security system. I figured you called."

Harper rolls his eyes. "We can't communicate. This has always been our problem, Seraphina. Jesus, you let a stranger into our house."

Harper is a master at making me feel like I'm to blame. I'm an awful mother, unfit to be at home, and I should go back to work immediately.

"Remember at the hospital, you said you would get us more security for the house? I was actually relieved that you finally did something right."

"Well, I wouldn't have if I didn't think you had scheduled the appointment. If I had thought I could even get you on the phone to answer my question, I might have called to check."

Belle, feeling the escalation of the fight, chimes in, "This isn't the time. We need you both to stay focused on the investigation for the sake of your child."

"Right, sorry," I say, my eyes blazing at Harper, the rage dark, desperate, and vulnerable. My worst fears are coming true.

"It's important we don't let any of this get out to the media. We need these people to think that Harper is still the prime suspect in the case. We are getting closer. Yao, can you talk Mrs. Swift through what we do have?" Lara says.

I can tell by the way she's looking at me that everyone in this room thinks I'm certifiable, totally insane. I wonder what Harper has told her.

"Your husband got another anonymous e-mail last night. The good news is even though it was sent through an anonymous retailer, he forgot to use a bridge, so all of the exit points are publicly listed. I know that means nothing to you, but for me, it's a jumping-off point to track and investigate."

I nod. My head is spinning.

Belle says, "An IP address isn't always a smoking gun, Yao."

"I know. I just need some more time to narrow things down."

At this point, all of the information feels like speculation. The newspapers and Internet chatter have made a strong case against Harper, incriminating him in the murder of Jessa Dante. The latest bizarre theory is a distorted lie that somehow seems plausible, the magic and illusion created by the spin of social media, stating that Harper is the Renaissance Killer and that he is responsible for all of the Boston murders, connected and triggered by the night of my attack, yet another gross and unsubstantiated theory flooding the airwaves.

I don't know who to believe.

The evidence is nothing more than anonymous e-mails, a series of offensive tweets, blasting out lies, and planting seeds of doubt against Harper. This investigation has crumbled into a bad game of telephone, our lives reduced to gossip, salacious stories, and cocktail banter.

"What did the e-mail say?" I say, spurred on by my intuition.

Belle lowers his head and lets out a deep sigh of resignation. Harper stands up and starts pacing, like an animal trapped in a cage.

After a moment, Belle says, "We were able to restore the hard drive of Jessa's computer and uncover most of her deleted files. Most of it was stuff for school or her business, PowerPoint presentations, and spreadsheets."

"She spent a lot of time on the Web," Yao says.

"I'm sure the dark web was a great place for her to grow her business," I say, unable to resist the jab.

Yao punches at the keyboard, and I watch as the browser opens up onto a website. The front page has an image of a butterfly, each wing in the shape of a skull with a red rose in the center, bloody and surrounded by sharp thorns.

"What is this?" I ask.

"They call themselves the Skull Club. They are anarchists, some sort of radical, stateless society. They put up names of individuals, hoping to incentivize murder. The bounty is collected in Bitcoin, a popular form of digital cash, and the retailers are all anonymous."

"Sort of like crowdfunding murder?" I ask.

"It's just another way to hire an assassin and cover your tracks. The fact that we have uncovered the site is going to be the breakthrough we need," Yao says.

"That's great but I'm not sure what any of this has to do with us."

She clicks on the rose, and it opens up another page, this one with only one name and a picture: Harper Swift

I don't know what to think when I see Harper's name. At first, I think this is madness. All of it, like some bad dream I will soon wake up from.

"Seraphina, can you remember anything else from that night you were attacked?"

Now it's all too real, and I'm terrified. My whole body freezes in fear. My mind spins, struggling to recover any of the lost details that may put an end to this darkness.

I think about my anxiety, night after night. Someone has been watching me, tracking us. The haunting begins after midnight; while the rest of the world sleeps, I lie awake, wide-eyed in fear. Death has been stalking my family, and it is dangerous and faceless, sheltered by the darkness.

All of this time, I have been made to feel as if my memories have evolved into some sort of madness, like witchcraft. These visions, these things I see and feel, are all real. They aren't just fragments of the past, trapped inside my mind.

I can hear the sound of my heart as it bangs inside my chest. Now I finally see the end, the sun that always rises, even after my darkest nights of pain and suffering. I can finally see the light.

The only thing that matters is our survival. I force myself to think about the attack, the hospital, anything that feels like a real memory, something other than the way his eyes looked that night before I was raped.

"My father was in the public eye. He didn't want anyone to know his daughter had been raped. He was embarrassed, and so was I."

"Your father didn't want you be become a victim all over again. He did it for you," Harper says.

"When are you going to stop defending my father and his shitty choices?"

"I'll keep working," Yao says. "Just be careful, Harp."

I don't feel like hiding; I feel strong. With the adrenaline and courage surging through me, I have found the resilience and the will to face the broken bones of my past, but this time I will win.

Harper takes my hand. "Let's go. Somewhere we can talk."

As we round the corner, a shadow falls over us. It's just the scaffolding from above, but I can feel the darkness of his blue eyes and hear the click of his black shoes against the pavement, just watching us, wherever we go.

Twenty Two
HARPER AND SERAPHINA

Some waves travel at the speed of sound, and as the speed increases, the waves are forced together, compressed. Eventually they collide, merging into a single shockwave, which travels at the speed of sound, faster, stronger, and invincible.

The threat of losing Harper, just the very thought of it, brings this moment into focus, giving me clarity and moving me forward with that same velocity.

The simple architecture of the Greenwich Inn fuses together our history, for us, a bridge connecting the past and present.

The slate-gray stone fireplace, mahogany shelves, and books line the walls of the penthouse. The light from the fireplace smolders. The reflection of it in my eyes is hypnotizing, a seductive dance.

Harper closes the door, and finally we're alone. "I'm sorry, Seraphina," he says.

"Me too."

"I should have believed you, but you've been acting so crazy."

"Carter said you were at the bar that night in Boston. It's all over the Internet. He made it seem like you were the one that attacked me," I say.

"I wasn't anywhere near the bar that night. Carter is a liar. You can't believe a word he says. I wish I had been there so that I could have saved you from all of that pain," he says. "I would have killed him, ripped him to pieces, and I would have enjoyed it. There's nothing I wouldn't do for you."

"I still love you, Harper. Nothing will ever change that. I don't know who to trust anymore," I say.

I can see now that I have been too stubborn, my words senseless, full of anger and hate. If I had not pushed my husband away, Jessa would not have squeezed into that small place inside his heart, a place meant only for me. This new threat to Harper's life scares me. I'm faced with losing him, and all of the pettiness, the failed expectations, the lies, his infidelity, all of the ills that can plague a marriage, have vanished. I still love him.

For Harper and me, our love is madness. His magic casts a spell, and nothing else seems to matter as long as we're together.

"I can't go home yet. I have to find out who is behind all of this. Go back to the house. Stay with Sky. You'll be safe there, and I don't want to have to worry about you," he says.

His hand lightly caresses the side of my cheek. I try to turn away. I run my hands through his hair. Harper looks at me, letting his desire take control of me. In my eyes, he can see that hunger, the passion and the desire, the divine inspiration that comes from being an artist.

"I need you," I say. "Come to bed."

He kisses me. His lips are soft and warm. His hands, unrestrained by fear, dominate me. I submit to the pleasure, and he worships me, as if I'm a goddess.

"My Maja," he whispers playfully in my ear, referring to his favorite painting from our trip to Madrid, *The Naked Maja* by Francisco Goya.

The model, naked and vulnerable, exposes herself without modesty or shame. Her arms placed behind her head in submission, her sex the center of the picture, on display. Her female gaze is fixed and fully aware of her erotic feminine power and the splendid enigma of it.

My body responds as he eases onto me and grabs my hips. I feel a quiver run through my body. The space between us is swallowed up in the sweetness of our release.

My heart is pounding, and the warmth surrounds us, affecting me like a potent drug.

"Sleep now," he says, kissing me, silencing my objections, until I drift away.

The sky has darkened, and the wind has picked up over the Hudson. The branches bend and sway, lashing out at each other.

Black clouds fill up the sky, an ominous warning, nothing like the rage of a powerful storm to come.

"A pack of Lucky Strikes," Harper says to the man behind the counter at the Rainbow Deli, as he fishes around in his gym bag for his wallet. He has been carrying around his laptop and everything else stuffed in there like a mobile office.

A bolt of lightning splits the sky, crackling and electric. As he walks, the streets are quiet, too quiet.

He lights a cigarette, takes a deep drag, and watches the tip flare up and the smoke swirl into the air.

Harper can feel someone behind him, as close as a shadow, and he reaches for his gun—which has been returned to him, along with his ID. As he crosses over the ramp of the parking garage, a car guns the accelerator.

A black van drives up on the sidewalk, side door wide open. Three bodies pile out, all wearing black military skull masks, glistening and metallic.

His mind is struggling to make sense of things, and all he can think is Seraphina.

In that moment, the adrenaline rips through his body, laced with regret and the knowledge that tonight is the night he is going to die.

Before Harper has the time to react, he feels the crack of metal against his skull, and the bitter taste of blood fills his mouth.

The color starts to fade from the world around him as he passes out.

Twenty Three
SERAPHINA AND CARTER

I don't know how much time has passed when the buzz from my cell phone jolts me out of a deep sleep. I open my eyes to find Harper gone. He didn't leave a note. He just vanished, as if the whole thing was just a dream. Heavy gray clouds crowd the light from the setting sun, and the sky is a deep, fiery red.

The text is from Carter:

* I need to see you. *

And then just two words:

* I remember.*

My stomach churns, my mind flashes, grasping at the bits and pieces from that night in Boston. It feels like Harper's time is running out, as if he is now being hunted, and the forces of evil are closing in around us. I dress quickly. I need to leave before Harper gets back, or else he will panic and convince me not to go see Carter, saying that Carter will have nothing to offer me but more lies. Harper will tell me it's too dangerous and that I belong at home with Sky.

I can't let him stop me. I have to speak to Carter; my intuition is telling me that he is the key to my disconnected past, and any details will help me put the pieces together and put an end to all of this madness and bloodshed.

The eyes that watch me, circling like a vulture up above, are making me feel like I'm insane.

All of Carter's lies about Harper—I need to set the record straight. The wind whips, and the rain thrashes outside against my window. The storm threatens to come inside. My mind spins, and anxiety floods my brain.

As I wait on the platform, the light at the end of the tunnel is only the Cannonball, a Hamptons express train out of Penn Station. I know that I'm being reckless by traveling alone, and I make sure no one is following me.

I feel the outline of the gun, and it brings me peace.

I panic and call Harper to tell him where I've gone and why I feel the need to be so impulsive, but he isn't picking up. I leave another message, feeling like I'm now stalking my husband.

The man across from me is reading the paper and keeps making furtive glances at me. I don't like him. I move to the back of the train, wishing I had my own laptop or something else to focus on, something other than my own fears and paranoia.

Next I try Belle, desperate for any new information, and letting him know I'm on my way to see Carter in Montauk and that he should call me immediately. I'm babbling. I leave a muddled message about Harper and how he has disappeared. I know that something awful has happened.

Who is driving this kill list and why?

I keep replaying all of the events, Brooke's murder and then Jessa's, going over the facts, trying to connect them back to that night in

Boston, the Renaissance Killer, and the Boston murders. My stomach twists in knots with a feeling that something is deeply wrong. It's gnawing at my insides.

It isn't like Harper to disappear, and I can't stop thinking of the worst-case scenario, that he has been kidnapped, beaten unconscious, needing my help, and I'm not there.

Or even worse, that he has been murdered, bloody and battered, and left like Jessa and Brooke.

I'm praying that everything is okay, but the rush of fear and anxiety is taking over, and I keep leaving messages on his phone.

"Harp, it's me. Call me back. I'm scared."

I keep leaving messages like this, over and over.

I'm feeling paralyzed and wishing I had gone home and waited, just like Harper told me to do. I never listen, a fact that pushes me further into a state of self-loathing.

I need to get off this train; the crush of people and the noise are making me feel claustrophobic. Aside from the single-lane traffic from hell, I prefer to drive to Montauk, through the potato fields, wide-open sky, and farmland, enjoying the serenity and tranquility of the water that surrounds me.

Finally, as the train pulls into the station in Montauk, I have to admit, I'm a mess.

I see Carter's black SUV, and his driver rushes over with an open umbrella as I step out of the train and onto the platform. I breathe a sigh of relief.

The panic in me starts to rise like mercury. The crescent moon hangs low in the night sky as we head toward Old Montauk Highway and the scenic bluffs of Carter's opulent mansion.

Twenty Four

HARPER

Harper opens his eyes, his breathing slow and weak, his body shaking, and his mind flooded with thoughts of Seraphina. He is alive but now held captive. The sound of men's voices and footsteps float up into the air, surrounding him.

"Move! Move!" a voice yells from behind him. He can feel the cold, hard metal point of an AK-47 at his back, and he can see the black military skull masks of his assailants out of the corner of his eye.

Harper has never known terror like this. His pulse thrashes in his ears, and his legs are weak. He reaches for his gun, but all that remains is an empty holster.

The emptiness of the space, an old warehouse, transformed into a masquerade, a kingdom of living darkness, swells with vice and chaos. Ghoulish faces on parade are anonymous, protected by their masks, all shadows of evil.

The room glows with wicked desire, like a ball on fire. He is pushed through a crowd of dancing, gyrating bodies, the walls around him pulsating to the beat of the electronic dance music. The room is tinted red.

A screen blasts images on the walls, and it's as if they pulsate with light and sound. In front of him, yellow lights glow, forming the shape of a pyramid, and then it shatters, fading into thirteen small temples of gold.

Harper realizes he must be hallucinating, as he passes a beautiful naked woman with a halo and wings on her back. The music, a requiem, pounds to the tribal beat, and to Harper, it feels like a dance of death, as if he has fallen into purgatory and is now surrounded by demons. The searing pain of his fear and anger takes over, and he is a prisoner in the panic of his own mind.

His vision starts to blur. His heartbeat feels like it's dangerously slow.

He is pushed forward into another room. The tiles on the floor are painted black and white, and in the center, spray-painted in colorful graffiti, is a pentagram.

A man is waiting for him, a black cloak covering his body and his face hidden by a mask. Harper shivers. It is cold and eerie, and the face of a goat with curved horns speaks to him. "Do you know why we've brought you here?"

"No," Harper says, his breathing weak.

"We believe you are guilty, possessed by an evil spirit, and we sentence you to a trial by ordeal."

Harper's mind is racing. He thinks of Brooke Beck, the brutality of her murder, and the remains of her body.

He closes his eyes and concentrates on Lara's words: "The seed of the Calabar bean is extremely poisonous; West African tribes used it as a system of law. They believed God would perform a miracle and let the accused live if they were innocent. If not, they died, an excruciating death from the poison, and justice was served."

Harper feels the blood rushing back into his body. His senses are raw and fragile, as if they are cross-wired, and he is seeing sounds as color, a deafening yellow, and tasting the bitterness of their words.

"We've given you an alkaloid poison, eserine. The effect is similar to nerve gas. Your heartbeat has already started to slow down, and some of what you see is just a hallucination. These are all side effects of the drug."

Harper can feel the hair on the back of his neck stand up.

"We are here to hold you accountable. Your survival will prove your innocence, or this will serve as your death sentence. The poison will draw out the truth, and it's your own guilt and sin that will destroy you," His tone is razor sharp.

"You people are fucking insane. This isn't justice. It's cold-blooded murder," says Harper, his rage flowing through him. "What did Helen Achlys do to deserve being drugged and hunted like an animal? Brooke Beck or Jessa Dante? How many others have you hunted and killed?"

"Matthew 15:19: For out of the heart come evil thoughts, murder, adultery, sexual immorality, theft, false witness, slander," he says. "We aren't afraid. We have faith in our God."

"You're never going to get away with this."

As Harper fades in and out, trapped in between two states of consciousness, he loses the words.

"We already have."

Harper is sick, thinking of the women, all victims, thrown away like trash. He can feel his blood boil; it flows through him, a river of searing anger and pain. He shuts down, saving his physical strength to fight the poison.

This is an evil beyond tolerance and reason, and one that only responds to the brutality of violence. He will find a way to live through this night, not only for Seraphina but also to seek retribution. He will not stop until people are free from these demons that haunt the earth.

Harper drops to his knees from the crippling nausea and is left alone to fight for his life.

Again, he thinks of Seraphina, their lost love and the sweetness of finding it all over again. He won't let anything come between them ever again, not in this life or in death. A child between them, Sky, will give their love wings and carry it forward with speed and grace.

To Harper, Seraphina will always be his eternal sunrise, an artist making poetry out of the mess and chaos, and his destiny.

The poison takes over, churning his insides and playing tricks on his mind. The pain starts to fade, a deep sleep takes over and seizes him, mind and body.

Harper's flashback shimmers, like an oasis of desert madness, and his childhood memories overwhelm him: the smell of whiskey, his father's fury, fueled by alcohol and addiction. All of it, making it harder for Harper to breathe.

His soul hangs heavy, weighted down, as if he is watching his own energy and life force drain from his body.

He feels disconnected.

His mind shifts into another vision, and he's a soldier at war, with a gun in his hand, firing a round of shots into the air, the sound of jazz against the backdrop of the brutality of war.

The broken rhythm of his dream continues, the drugs forcing the images to layer, one on top of the other, slowing his pulse even further.

Again, he's a young boy, chasing an eagle, through the courtyard of the projects toward home. He throws open the door and climbs the stairs, hearing the hauntingly familiar sounds of fighting and his mother sobbing. The pain of it all, still real, is etched deeply in his mind, flowing through him, hot like lava, burning everything it touches.

He hears the sound of a gunshot and watches his father fall to the ground, arms flailing. He keeps falling, through the earth and into a shallow grave.

Harper looks up to find his mother holding the smoking gun, trembling and crying, gripped by fear and desperation after killing his father.

Harper takes the gun from her and the guilt of her crime, all in his own hands and heart.

These visions are hard, wrapped up in the guilt, pain, and loneliness of his lost childhood.

Now he can hear the music pulsing through him, the weight of the trauma crushing down, and he knows he is dying.

He watches as the face of his mother starts to fade, and in her place stands Seraphina, bruised and beaten.

His mind twisting even further, he hears the sound of another shot, although this time, in the darkness of his mind, he can see it's Seraphina pulling the trigger.

Harper doesn't have the strength to go to her, and all he can do is cry out in pain.

Seraphina is fire, and each time she touches the earth, it's as if she sets it on fire with her pain. Only she could have found a way to melt the frozen walls around his heart with her heat and desire.

The door opens, and Harper can't tell if he is hallucinating. He is starting to lose consciousness. The dark figure locks the door and moves closer to him and removes the hood. It's Jessa.

His vision is blurred and the sound of her voice forces him to focus.

Jessa takes his hand and puts it up to her face and says, "I am alive. It's me, Jessa. Stay with me, Harper. The only antidote to the poison they have given you is atropine. I'm going to give it to you now, and it will save your life. We are still in danger. You have to follow me. I can get you out safely."

Harper nods.

She injects him with a syringe.

In the distance, he thinks he can hear the sound of sirens, and they're getting closer, howling like a pack of wolves.

Twenty Five

SERAPHINA AND CARTER

Carter is waiting for me outside the house. The glow from the candlelight and fiery metal torches illuminates the grounds of the estate. The flames dance against the hypnotic lull of the surf and the smell of saltwater.

In the distance, the melody of a child's laughter, bright and sweet, carries like a wind chime.

The storm has passed, and the Montauk sky is clear, a patchwork of stars and light. The moon hangs over the pool, its reflection a shimmering silver streak cutting through the crystal blue water. For Carter and me, magic still exists between us, as if in some past life, we connected deeply, and then the chain was violently broken. Now our fates are once again colliding.

We walk through the house. The doors and windows rattle, as the wind drives out the last few raindrops from the storm.

"Can I get you a drink?" Carter says, pouring himself a glass of red wine.

"Sure. I would love some wine," I say, feeling awkward and uneasy, my mind still obsessing over Harper.

I'm not sure what is wrong with me. Now that I'm here, I'm desperate to be there. I can't stand not knowing if Harper is all right. What will happen if I can't find out anything useful from Carter? Will we be forced to live in a state of constant terror? I can tell Carter is in a dark and intense mood. I regret my decision to come here even more now, a feeling that is totally useless.

For Carter, falling in love is a maelstrom of passion and a power struggle that he will always win. I have to consider that this is all a game to him and remember that he is a master of manipulation.

My intuition tells me to stay sharp and focused.

There's something about Carter; like a sorcerer, he draws me in, magnetic and ethereal. He has charm and charisma, an unquantifiable and unpredictable piece of human chemistry and one that helps him teach and achieve true magic, suspended and without wires.

"You know, even though you drive me mad, I've never stopped thinking about you," Carter says. He reaches out and puts his hand over mine.

"I stopped sending you letters, but I never stopped writing them. I want you to read one," he says, pushing a pile of notes toward me. "Go ahead, just one." He stares at me disconcertingly.

The light from the candle flickers. It casts an eerie glow.

Seraphina,

You dazzle, even in your grief and pain; I tried to heal your wounds. I tried to kiss the parts that were broken, and through that love, both of us were reborn, transformed into living gold.

I love to watch you think, the beauty of your mind, always twisting and turning, firing on all cylinders.
As if, overnight, you became my religion, a sanctuary for my pain and pleasure. I tried to forget you.
Your love left a scar—a poisonous wound that won't heal. I can't forget you. And without you, I can't live. The light has gone out, and I find myself consumed by darkness.

Eternally yours,
Carter

I let the silence take over the moment, seeing the depth of his love for the first time and the darkness of his passion.

I have the sensation that the world is spinning, as if I'm on a merry-go-round that moves faster and faster, so fast that you've missed the moment where you could have jumped off and survived the fall with only a few bumps and bruises.

"Carter, I love Harper. I always have."

The look on his face is distraught, his pain all too real and his heart breaking.

I inadvertently knock his wine glass over, spilling it on his white shirt, now stained red, dripping onto the floor like drops of blood.

"Jesus, Seraphina," he shouts, standing up, filled with rage and fury just blazing at me, his whole body coiled as if he is ready to strike. All of it reminds me of the night I was attacked.

My mind flashes, the echo of footsteps; again my heart is pounding. The pain that comes in quick cuts and the force of the blows. Violence is hell, sharp like razor blades.

I'm energy and light, free from the pain, coursing through my body. I recede into a jigsaw puzzle of noises and fragmented images, now stored in the hard drive of my memory. I can taste the blood in my mouth.

SEEING RED

It has been such a strange and tiring day. It must be my anxiety about Harper's disappearance triggering the flashbacks.

Carter senses my fear and gathers his emotions, although something is still smoldering beneath the surface. He takes his shirt off, still wet with wine. His eyes are fixed on me, letting me see his strength and dominance and the chiseled lines of his stomach.

I think of his body on me; our sex was always charged with an electric tension, like wild animals, intense and primitive. As if the spirit of war flows through Carter, deep within his soul.

I notice he has a single teardrop tattoo on his back. I've never seen it before. I'm disconnected. My chest is heavy. I fight to breathe.

I can hear that voice again inside my head, just barely a whisper, saying, "It's too late to be out in the dark alone. What a mess you are. What a mess you will be."

"Your tattoo, does it mean something?" I say, pointing to it, giving me time to collect my thoughts and to calm my fears before they overwhelm me.

"My mother and I were very close. I was devastated when she chose to take her own life. She had so much to live for. The teardrop reminds me of that loss," he says.

"Oh, my God. I'm so sorry."

"I'm just kidding. You should have seen the look on your face. I got drunk one night in Vegas and woke up with it," he says with a grin.

He laughs, that same blend of charm, tension, and evil wit to defuse his sharp edges.

I laugh, an uncomfortable laugh. I don't trust him.

This is all a game to him. He enjoys keeping me off balance. Carter is in an awful mood tonight, his darkness on display. I have seen his cruelty and misogyny before. He likes to push me to the edge. It throws him into some sort of perverted ecstasy. He is intoxicated by the imbalance of power.

From the kitchen, the teapot on the stove starts to scream, and I jump. Carter goes to the kitchen to get my tea.

I try calling Harper but still get no answer. I send a text to Jacob. *I need help.*

Carter comes back and sits down quietly.

He says, "I've got all of this, Seraphina. The one thing I haven't been able to have is you. I want for us to finally be a family. Sky is beautiful and strong, you know. Just like you," Carter says, standing above me with a kettle of steaming hot water.

My anxiety rising. It's been hours since I've slept, my legs are shaky. I can't keep running and hiding. I can't think rationally. I just *need* to think.

I try to make up an excuse.

"I have to call home and check on the baby."

I dial Harper's number again as I walk. It goes to voice mail. *I text. Help me. Where are you?*

I have no idea where I'm going. I just keep walking down the hall and opening doors. I reach for my gun. My mind is spinning, flashing back to my nightmares. The door takes me into the study. In a glass case, I see hunting knives, ammunition, and guns. I run my fingers over the glass; my eyes rest on the arrows and spears.

From behind me comes his voice: "Silly girl, you're lost. It's just a hobby. Don't let it frighten you."

I keep walking and find the bathroom. I shut the door behind me. It's clean and modern, like the rest of the house. It feels more like a sterile hospital room. I'm pacing, trying to think straight. I need to come up with a plan. Carter must sense my fear. I need to get out of the house.

SEEING RED

I look in the mirror, tracing the lines of my jagged scar. For me, perfect doesn't exist; it's unreal, bland and untouchable.

My reflection is darker, with broken pieces exposed, raw and fused together, the same ones that have brought my life into sharper focus.

These are the scars that drive me forward, a constant reminder that I'm a survivor.

My mind is spinning. The flashbacks layer one on top of the other, burying me with the weight of it. I think of Sky, and I hear a whisper, "Hickory dickory dock, the mouse ran up the clock."

I call Belle and he answers on the first ring.

"Seraphina, I've been trying to reach you. Harper's missing." His voice is overly anxious and eager to speak to me.

"What happened?" My voice trembles.

Belle says, "We don't know. We will find him."

The slow drip of the memories flow, now a torrent of pain, tearing me into pieces. I hold back the tears. I need Carter to believe I am still in control. "Where are you, Seraphina?"

"I'm in Montauk, with Carter." My eyes are burning and my voice unsteady.

"You know you are your own worst enemy. We told you to stay at home with Sky. Get out of that house. You are in danger."

Carter starts banging on the door, and I drop the phone and reach for my gun.

"Come out now. We have to talk," he says, still throwing his full weight against the door. I can see it start to give.

"I can explain everything," he says, breaking through the door.

I'm frozen with fear.

I can see his face behind me. As I turn my head to look in the mirror, he kisses me, and his hands travel up my body. He takes my gun away, putting it out of my reach.

He says, "She's mine. Isn't she? Sky is my child. You have no right to keep her from me. I told you I wasn't ready to let you go. I warned you."

I remember now, screaming without sound. His body crushing me.

"I love you, Seraphina. I'm sorry. I was angry when you left me, so quickly and for no good reason. I hired someone to hurt you, but he wasn't supposed to hurt you that badly."

Something wooden, heavy as a baseball bat, cracks my skull. No more pain.

The images are coming back to me. I remember hearing a man sobbing. Begging. Moaning. Dragging.

"Just enough so that you would come back to me. That way, I could take care of you and be the hero. And I did. I picked you up. I put you back together again. I'm so sorry. He wasn't supposed to rape you. I had to kill him. I saved you. I've always wanted to protect you. That child is mine."

I let the rage fill me up and flow through me, giving me purpose and strength to fight and win.

My mind is clear and ready now. I focus on the moment, staying calm and breathing, sharp and focused.

"What is this loyalty you have to your husband? He cheated on you. He thinks you're crazy. He's made everyone around you think you are insane and an unfit mother. Nobody will believe you."

"What did you do to Harper?" I ask as I slam my elbow into his neck, knocking the wind out of him. He falls backward onto a glass shelf, shattering it into pieces.

I still can't get to my gun, so I put my hands up in front of me, ready to fight.

I say, "It's not Harper. It's you. You have been behind all of this. You were watching me from that boat. You made me think I was going crazy. You almost destroyed everything, my life and my marriage."

He smiles and puts his hand up to his eyebrow, shocked to see that I've made him bleed.

"It's nice to see you fight back this time, not just lie there like you did that night. It's much more interesting this way," he says.

Carter is on his feet now, using his shoulder and charging into me, snapping his head forward, toward the bridge of my nose, splitting it open.

I'm not fast enough, and the blow delivers a burning pain in my head. I fall backward, reaching for something to grab as I go down.

I repeat, "What have you done to Harper?"

"You're such an ungrateful bitch and so naive. You're also a horrible mother. You were stupid enough to let a stranger into your house to install a security system. That's right. Remember Johnny. He should be at your house right now. You can't win. He's just waiting for one word from me and you will never see your family again. Maybe you're just a stupid whore like the rest of them," he says, and then he's on top of me, his hands around my neck, and I'm choking.

I have to make him think I've given up. I let all of the color drain from my face.

"This is all your fault. If you'd just stayed with me, we wouldn't be in this position. That is my child, and I want to help you raise her. I want for us all to finally be a family. Please, Seraphina. I love you."

In my mind, I hear Jacob saying, "A strike to the eyes can disable an opponent who is choking you, quickly and effectively."

My head spins, and my mouth fills with blood. I am not weak. I will not give up. I will fight back.

I pluck at his eyes with my fingers. Carter's gaze falls upon me, and my blood runs cold. Without his colored lenses, his eyes are different colors, one watery, black like a vulture's eye, and one blue. My mind flashes back to my nightmares and I'm staring into the eyes of a madman. I make up my mind to win and to rid myself of his gaze forever.

"I guess it's time you see the real me," Carter says, his mouth twisting into an evil smile. "I'm completely blind in one eye. My father was a chemist. This is what happens when you play with poison."

Poison. My senses are heightened. My mind is on overload. Carter is a killer and a sociopath. He is responsible for the murders of Brooke Beck and Jessa Dante. He is behind all of these murders. He camouflaged his crime with a corpse that night in Boston, but he is the killer. I wasn't sure how many women he had raped and murdered. He's speaking to me now, but I can't hear anything. The world's gone dark again, black as the vulture that's been circling above me. Black as the night I was attacked.

For a second, I'm dazed by the ferocity of the attack, and then I realize blood is trickling down my forehead into my eyes. My head is throbbing and I think I'm going to be sick. He ties a rope around my waist and drags me toward the bed. I'm lying down, groaning in pain, like an animal. He's leaves me in the dark.

I struggle to break free, and in the process, I knock over a lit candle on his nightstand and watch as the flame crawls along the floor and up the curtains.

I reach for my gun, but he kicks it further away. "You should be thanking me for getting rid of Harper. He just wanted you for your money."

"That's not true. You've been making me think I'm crazy. You sent Jessa. You're behind all of this. Where is Harper?"

"Harper did this to himself. He's always been so obsessed with truth and justice. It clouds his judgment. He deserves a trial. Although we all know he's guilty until proven innocent."

I'm stunned. The fire is edging closer, and I can't hold back my tears.

"Have you ever heard of the Skull Club. They also believe in truth and justice."

"I'm going to ask you one more time. Where is Harper? I'll never choose you. I hate you, Carter. You will never have me or my family."

"He was given an alkaloid poison, eserine. The effect is similar to nerve gas. It's a horrible way to die, but eventually his heart will just stop beating. Isn't that poetic? Your Romeo will die of a broken heart. Without me, you're left with nothing, Seraphina. I can give you the world. I have money and power. All I want is you. You have to make the right choice, or I promise, I'll destroy you."

"I don't need you or your protection. You're the devil, Carter."

"And you're an ungrateful whore."

"Your mother didn't commit suicide and it wasn't an accident. Was it? You poisoned her. And you killed Brooke Beck and Jessa to frame Harper. How many other women have you murdered?"

"You can't win. I'll never let you go."

Carter is hurt badly; blood runs from his eye. He tries to get to his feet but falls back down.

"I'll go to the police. I'll take out a restraining order."

"Nobody will believe you. They all think you're crazy. I've made sure of that. You didn't help with all of your drinking and the medication. You won't get a restraining order, and you will never get to be a mother. It's a good deal. Take it, and no one will ever know. With Harper out of the way, we can finally live happily ever after."

My blood is rising, and the adrenaline takes over. I'm soaring. Again I hear Jacob's voice: "Own the moment. Fight to win. You will not be a victim."

I imagine the fire engulfing Carter, dragging him down as he falls into the depths of hell.

"You're right. We will be happy together. We'll be a family. You, me, and Sky."

He can't see anything. He moans loudly. I edge closer to the gun.

"I love you Carter. I always have."

I feel my fingers wrap around the coldness of the steel grip.

I have six bullets and I fire each one at his head. The smoke and fire are rising up around me. I run down the steps, out the front door, and into the night air. My whole body is trembling, bloody and weak.

I keep running, and it feels like time is crawling, with the chaos of the waves crashing and the lighthouse in the distance; all sound and no picture.

I turn back finally to see the house engulfed in flames. The blood-red sky slashed with dark clouds of gray smoke. The flames rise higher, scorching the hollowed-out darkness at the center.

The whole Montauk sky is lit up like fireworks on the Fourth of July.

For me, for the first time, I feel safe, now firmly anchored to the earth, like the boats in the harbor.

All along, I believed the world was a dark place, filled with things to fear and hide from, one that I was forced to face alone.

I realize now, as I watch my nightmares turn to ash, that the light was there all along, just hidden from me by the darkness of what happened that night in Boston.

I have the truth, and my mind feels free and clear. There are no more shadows on the horizon.

By the time the emergency crew arrives, the house is nothing more than dust and glowing embers.

I close my eyes and everything slowly fades to black.

And all I can see in front of me is Harper with a bright and radiant Sky.

Acknowledgment

I am grateful to the following people for their help and support:

To my husband, my rock for reading and editing every draft and for his love and passion.

And to my daughter, Caylin, and my son, Logan, your love is my everything.

To my mother, my earth angel, for her endless capacity to love and support my dreams.

And to my father for his love and strength, who taught me the value of hard work, leading by example.

To Ken, thank you for your friendship and support.

To Michelle Raimo, Meryl Poster and Arianna Huffington, trailblazing women who believe and continue to inspire me.

To Deb, Stacey, Lisa and Alison, for their love and laughter, and often yanking me back to real life.

I am eternally grateful to Dr. Ned Hallowell, a friend and mentor, who helps so many find a safe place in the world.

Author Biography

Heidi Brod is a former Film executive, wife and mother of two based in New York City. This is her first thriller. She has been an active part of the New York Film community and always dreamed of writing stories that readers would fall in love with.

Printed in the United States
By Bookmasters